BY
PARKER ALBERTS

WITH
JEMMA BIXBY

Room for One More?

Simon flipped the card over and followed the directions. Now he was standing at the window of a motel room in the south part of town. He wasn't sure why he was there, but the card made it seem important. He twisted the band on his finger. Simon leaned closer. The light filtered through the crack in the curtain enough that he saw two shapes moving around. Women. One was blonde, and the other was a redhead. He pressed into the side of the building. He glanced around to be sure this wasn't a set up for an episode of Punk'd. There wasn't anyone else, just him. The curtains fluttered, and he saw a petite hand push them open a little more.

Lacy and Jane knew that Simon was interested in both of them. They also knew his wife was straight-laced and would never agree to share him. They were an odd couple. He was the punk rock chic guy, and she was stiff, everything by the book. They had no children that Lacy knew of. So, she mailed a card to Simon and set up this "meeting."

Lacy and Jane had been lovers off and on for the last year or so. They were both a bit wild and loved to fuck men and women. So, here they found themselves. Both dressed to please the other. Lacy was dressed as a Japanese schoolgirl, and Jane was dressed as an elf. Standing in full view of the window, they stepped closer to each other. They looked each other up and down, approving.

Lacy reached up and caressed Jane's face. Then, she leaned in and kissed her on the lips. It was a soft, gentle kiss. Jane responded by pulling Lacy in close, holding her. Their hands wandered, exploring body parts, fondling and caressing breasts. Jane, wanting to feel Lacy quiver, paid attention to her nipples under the tight cloth of her shirt. She dropped her mouth to it and began to suck. Lacy stroked Jane's hair.

"I want your mouth on my skin," she whispered.

Jane lifted the sailor-style shirt, popped open the front closure bra, and fed hungrily on Lucy's nipple. She gripped Lacy's back and gently laid her back on the bed.

Simon peered through the slit in the curtain. He stifled a gasp because he knew these women. He'd seen them a lot in the corner store. They were both beautiful, and he'd inquired about them. He'd been dreaming of sinking his cock into both of them. Now he knew they weren't that way. But he would get off just watching them.

Jane slid Lacy back, so her behind was just at the edge of the bed. She left her breasts exposed to the air. Trailing kisses down to her clean-shaven pubic bone, Jane lifted Lacy's skirt and kissed her. She plunged her tongue into her pussy and kissed Lacy like it was her mouth, tasting her. She pulled her tongue out and licked her clit intently, occasionally slipping her tongue into her.

Lacy grabbed at Jane's hair, "Not yet! This wasn't... oh God. Oh God! Jane, wait. I don't want to come yet!"

Jane slowed and stopped.

"I'm sorry. I love when you move against my face. I can't help myself!" Jane replied.

Lacy sat up and pulled her top off, her bra hung down. Jane slipped the bra off and kissed the tops of her breasts. Lacy cupped her chin, kissing Jane, tasting herself on her lover's lips and tongue. She pulled her up onto the bed, and they lay down. Lacy stroked Jane's body.

These women were arousing him, and Simon could feel his dick getting hard against the fabric of his pants. Soon, he'd have to fuck them, or he'd have to masturbate right here. He shot a look around and didn't feel comfortable. Simon turned back to the window.

Lacy was in the process of undressing Jane. She'd worn something short with a pair of bracers and a leather bodice. The bodice was open with an ample bosom spilling out. Lacy was straddling Jane, massaging her breasts as she rocked against Jane's hips. Jane wriggled underneath the wetness of Lacy's pussy. Lacy leaned down, caught Jane's nipple in her mouth, bit down and pulled. Jane tensed up. Her nails dug into Lacy's thighs. She tugged at her, urging her to go down. Taking the nudge, she slid down, propped Jane's legs on her shoulders, and set to work. She licked Jane's lips and clit, stroking them faster and faster. She plunged her tongue in and out, alternating between licking and flicking her swollen clit.

Simon could barely stand the tension. He tried the door and discovered that it was unlocked. He pushed it open. Slowly, he approached. Jane, in the throes of passion, noticed him and pushed Lacy's head back. She looked up, turned her head, and motioned for

Simon to come to the bed. The women could see the hardness bulging in his pants.

They pulled him onto the bed, conveniently king size. They undressed him and tied down his hands and feet. Lacy and Jane both laid down and paid great attention to his throbbing manhood. Each stroked and sucked him in turn. They would stop when they thought he was going to come. Lacy straddled him and lowered herself onto his waiting cock. Jane straddled his face. Her pussy already wet, he stroked her clit and worked furiously to taste her juices as Lacy rode him, holding onto Jane's breasts.

Jane grabbed Lacy's hands and played with her nipples.

"Do you want his dick? It fits so well," Lacy asked Jane.

"No, I want you to fuck me, and I want him to suck my tits," she panted.

She removed herself from his face. Lacy slid off his cock.

"Hmm, I want him to fuck me some more. But I want to fuck you! How will we manage?" Lacy asked.

Jane fished around in a bag between the bed and the wall. She pulled out a flesh-colored dildo. Attached to it was a leather harness with buckles. Simon pulled against his restraints.

"It's okay, Simon. It's not for you," she said as she strapped it on, "it's for Jane."

Jane untied Simon.

"Wow, I want to be inside both of you," he replied.

Jane bent over a chair, legs spread, and Lacy inserted the fake dick. She pushed in and pulled out, moving back and forth. She rammed in hard.

Simon searched the bag and found a condom. He slipped it on and grabbed Lacy as she was pumping away. She continued to move as he entered her. They moved awkwardly at first but fell into a rhythm. Jane reached down and rubbed her clit. Lacy clutched Jane's hips. Simon clutched Lacy's hips as he pumped in and out of her back door. She gripped Jane tighter. Jane cried out as she orgasmed and lost strength in her arms. Lacy pulled the dripping dick out. She stops Simon.

"Pull out and take the condom off," she said, "I want your cock in my pussy. Jane can do what she wants."

Simon complied. Lacy laid down on the bed. He propped her legs up on his shoulders and sunk deep into her wet, warm cavern. He started slowly, moving in and out. Jane curled up on the bed, watching. He thrust in harder and faster.

"Deeper Simon, come on, I want you to fill all of me with your cock," Lacy gasped.

Simon pushed as deep as he could and used short, fast strokes to stay there. She tilted her hips up more. She gasped and moaned louder.

"Simon, faster, harder!"

He shoved, rammed and thrust as fast and as hard as he could. He was rewarded with warmth, flooding over his dick before he released into her. She shuddered and went limp. He pulled out and bent down to her pussy. He slid his tongue over her clit and felt her shake again. He tasted his juices mixed with his own.

Gently, he lowered her down to the bed. He slipped his arms around her, and Jane slid over. The three of them curled up and drifted off to sleep.

Dream of Me

Jessie stood in front of the full-length mirror. She'd just gotten back from an interview, and she studied herself. Of course, they had been very specific in the manner of dress. She had followed the directions. So what went wrong? She inventoried herself for the hundredth time today.

Hair pulled back into pigtails, high on her head; white button-up shirt; red and black striped tie; red, black and white plaid pleated skirt; white knee high socks; and last but not least, killer heels that looked like old fashioned schoolmarm shoes. Everything was right. What was wrong?

Jessie traced the collar of her shirt lightly with her fingertips. Her fingers brushed the pale skin of her throat. She sighed. She had been the only redhead in a sea of blondes and brunettes. She picked up the remote, hoping to drown her sadness in the beat of the music. She had no recollection of what was actually in the CD player. The song she had rehearsed for the interview resided in her laptop and her mp3 player.

She cheered up when she heard the melody of Madonna's "Erotica" floating out of the speakers. It was her favorite. Jessie still stood in front of the mirror. She closed her eyes and let the music move her. The skirt flipped and spread out as she moved her hips to the chorus "I'd like to put you in a trance all over, erotic, erotic, put your hands all over my body. Erotic, erotic." Her hands traversed the fabric of her shirt. It stretched snugly across her chest.

Jessie's favorite past time was dancing. She closed her eyes and imagined what it would be like to have the kind of body and fearlessness to dance in front of men, half-naked, in a gentlemen's club. She wasn't naïve. She knew that they were all strip clubs. She knew it wasn't a genuinely great ambition, but it was a good living if you were good at it. Instead, shy little Jessie took to bartending.

There was a knock at her door shattering her imaginary stage. She looked out the peephole and nearly squealed with excitement. Jessie threw the door open and wrapped her arms around the man that stood there. She didn't even let him put his bags down.

Spencer dropped the bags and wrapped the young woman in a hug as best he could. He kissed her on the forehead and breathed in the fragrance of her hair.

"Damn, I missed you," he whispered.

" Me too," she mumbled. She loosened her grip, "Don't ever leave me again."

"I won't. I promise. Now, can we get inside? I would love to give old Ms. Troupe a show but not when I'm a bit rusty."

"Oh baby, just take me right here," she replied.

Spencer released a low growl, "Don't tempt me."

Jessie pressed into him and ran a hand over his backside. She grabbed hold and pulled him into her. She could feel his reaction.

"Hm, he's hungry. I suggest we feed him."

Spencer kissed her and wasting no time, his tongue in her mouth exploring hungrily. How he'd missed the warmth of her welcoming mouth, and now, he remembered why he'd remained faithful. He slowly walked her back until her back pressed into the door casing. Her hand slipped under his shirt, and her nails dug into his flesh. He moaned into her mouth.

Jessie broke away. She stared into his brown eyes, and he gazed back into her blues. He put his right hand against the wall. She slid down, unbuttoning her top as she went until it was hanging open. He glanced down and saw the tops of her breasts peeking out of a black lace bra. He reached for them and had his hand slapped. She unzipped his pants, reached in and found what she was after.

She pulled out his hard unit. Teasingly, she kissed the head and the shaft. Then she ran her tongue slowly and lightly over his cock. Her hand gripped the base, and she took him into her mouth. Jessie worked him in and out of her mouth. She moved her hand up, gently squeezing and twisting on the way. Only the tip was in her mouth now. Her tongue traced circles around the rim as she gently sucked. She could feel herself getting wet.

"Oh God," he whispered.

Jessie let his hardness slip from her mouth. She unfastened her bra. Still holding Spencer's dick in her hand, she pressed it against her warm skin. She held her breasts together, enveloping him and moved up and down. He rocked his hips as if he was inside, fucking her. She could tell he was close to release. She stopped cold. She slid back up him.

"How was that for giving everyone a show?" she asked. She took one of his bags and reentered her apartment, leaving Spencer and his dick exposed.

Grunting, Spencer hefted the remaining bag and followed her. He dropped the bag inside the door, shut and locked it. No interruptions, not after being gone this long.

Jessie had gone back to her mirror. A chair sat in front of it. Her music still played. "Everybody's talkin' 'bout wanting that and needing this. I'd just like to know if you'd like to learn a different kind of kiss. So won't you, go down where it's warm inside. Go down, where I cannot hide. Go down, where all life begins. Go down, that's where my love is."

She was swaying and moving to the music. Spencer stepped up behind her, she shifted and felt his hardness still out in the open. She rolled her hips and let the fabric caress him. He grabbed her breasts and pulled her tightly to him.

" It's not nice to tease," he whispered in her ear.

"So? You teased me with every phone call, every letter," was her reply.

One of Spencer's hands slipped down her stomach to the clasps that held her skirt. With a practiced hand, he undid them and let it slide to the floor, exposing matching black lace panties. He caressed the soft material and felt the heat from between her legs. He kissed her neck and gently bit her. She bent her head to the left and leaned back, exposing more of her throat. He bit her harder, and she gasped.

He slid his hand between her thighs and cupped her. He smiled. He could feel the moisture soaking through the fabric. He pushed the material aside and slipped a finger inside her. Jessie was already slick. It would make it easier to slide his ready cock into her. He pulled his finger out and gently drug it up to her clit. He stroked her. She moaned. His other hand still clutched her covered breast. He pushed the fabric of her shirt and bra aside. He massaged it, and she pressed back into him.

"Damn you, Spencer. Just fuck me," Jessie demanded.

Spencer released her. She spun around, she stepped back a little, and with her foot, she shoved him into the chair. She smiled. His dick was hard and standing ready for her. She slipped off her panties and left them piled on top of her skirt. She swung one leg over and lowered herself down onto his soldier.

"It's been too long. You feel so good inside me baby," she whispered as she rolled her hips.

"Agreed," he responded as he took a nipple into his mouth. He sucked it and teased it with his tongue. He felt Jessie's muscles tighten around his dick. He bit down, and she squirmed.

Jessie wrapped her legs around him. He gripped her and stood up from the chair. Spencer sunk to his knees and laid her back on the floor. He placed her legs on his shoulders and started thrusting into her. Her fingernails dug into the skin on his chest urging him to go faster.

"Harder," she moaned, "Deeper."

Spencer slowed his strokes and pushed deeper into her.

"Oh God," she whispered.

Spencer went faster, harder and deeper, "Damn. You feel so good."

"Spencer, oh my God," she moaned louder, "Spencer!" She dug her nails into his shoulders and arched her back, her body pressing to him. The friction on her clit was becoming too much she orgasmed and cried out.

Spencer kept thrusting into her and kissing her face, "Can I come in you?"

"Oh God yes, yes. I want to feel you in me."

A few more thrusts and Spencer released inside of her.

" Spencer lay here. I want to feel you inside of me," Jessie said and kissed him deeply. She was still feeling orgasmic and wanted to feel her lover inside her.

He collapsed on top of her, and she moved a little.

"You need some help?"

"I want all the little ones too," she replied.

He pulled out of her and lifted her hips, "Bend your legs, like you're going to sit on my shoulders."

Jessie did as instructed, and her pussy was just inches from Spencer's face. He could feel the heat; smell the sex. His tongue caressed her, taking in all of the liquid they had made. She bucked against his face as she orgasmed again and again. He could tell from her body's movements how powerful each one was until she slowed and sighed.

Gently, he lowered her to the floor. He leaned over and kissed her. Her hands slipped around his head, and she deepened the kiss wanting to taste her on him. It was moments like this when she knew that there could never be another one that satisfied her like this.

But there had been another while Spencer was away. She had an appetite that was quite difficult to manage. As they laid in each other's arms and drifted off to sleep, Jessie thought about her other lover.

It had been just a couple of months after Spencer's confusing departure. She had been flirting with one of the guys at a club where she hung out. They had gotten intense, and after a few messages back and forth on their cell phones, Jessie couldn't stand it. She put the offer out that he should come over and she never expected him to accept. But he did and later that afternoon he appeared at her doorstep.

He was tall and lean. He was young compared to Jessie, but he spoke to her in a very straightforward manner, and she liked it. Some days she just needed to have a man tell her he wanted to fuck her. He did that. He'd flirted and hinted and she'd not taken it seriously. After all, she was madly in love with Spencer.

Jin was a nice guy, and Jessie liked to look at him. He was easy on the eyes. She knew she had more experience and told him there were things she could teach him; she'd be glad to help. He arrived on her doorstep, and she led him inside, straight to her room and her bed.

He kissed her after stripping down to his boxers. She gladly returned the kiss. He'd pushed her back and with little direction turned his attention to her breasts, still encased in her bra and she gave him his first lesson. She popped open her bra, it was a front closure and opened easily letting her spill out. Her nipples were erect. As soon as his mouth covered one of them she could feel the moisture starting to seep out from her. The gentle sucking made her wet. She wanted another kiss but the limited time required they get right to it.

Jin had asked her to ride him, and she was happy to oblige. Jessie had him lay on the bed, and after rolling the condom on his long hard cock, she lowered herself down. It felt good to have a man inside her how she craved and longed for it. Jessie needed a cock. She thought she could live without one and here was proof that she was wrong. As she slid him in and out, she pressed into him, making sure that she got off too. It wouldn't do to get him off and not her. The look of pleasure on his face and his hands on her ass were keeping her hot. She wanted more.

Had there been a time she would have shown him the things she would have done to his hard manhood. After he left her company, she imagined the next time they could hook up. She imagined what it would feel like in her mouth, the warm skin, the taste of his flesh. She wanted to feel him pulsing against her tongue as she slid him in and out. She felt the need to hold him in her hands and stroke him.

Jessie wanted to suck him and wanted to feel his cum on her skin, against her breasts. She wanted to show him what it was like with a woman who enjoyed her work. Jessie drifted off to sleep thinking of Jin and wanting to fuck him. They never had the chance to do it again.

Lady Becca

Becca walked down the street when she took notice of a man sitting at an outdoor café ahead of her. She sat down across from him and pretended to be a little faint.

"Are you okay?" he asked as she fanned herself.

"Why, yes. I think I will be. You don't mind if I sit here a moment, do you?" Becca responded as she grabbed a napkin and wiped off imaginary sweat.

"Uh, no, not at all."

Becca gave him a winning smile and continued wiping "sweat" from her neck. She slowly drew the napkin down to the opening of her shirt and patted the swelling tops of her breasts. She was wearing a low cut tank top and a thigh-length denim skirt. Her bra was peeking out.

The young man's eyes traveled from Becca's face to her hand. They followed her hand, and their gaze rested on her breasts. She leaned forward and pushed them up slightly with her arms. His eyes were fixated on them.

"What's your name?" she asked.

"Joe," he replied.

"Joe? Hm, well, Joe, I have a problem. You are the solution to my problem."

"Really? And what's the problem?"

"I need your dick?"

Joe was stunned for a moment, "Say that again?"

"I want to fuck you. Now, right here."

Becca rose and sat in Joe's lap. She leaned forward, her breasts inches from his face. He buried his face in them.

"Just go with it," Becca said.

She stroked his hair and pushed his head further into her breasts.

"Bite me," she whispered forcefully. She pushed her hips down and wriggled against Joe's cock. She slid her body down under the table. She was oblivious to the slowly gathering crowd.

"What's your name?" Joe asked as he heard the zipper of his pants go down.

"Becca," she responded.

He felt her hands, one around the base of his shaft, the other in his pants on his hip. Her fingernails dug into his flesh. She licked the tip of his dick and put it in her mouth, gently sucking.

She moved her hand up and down, stroking him. Becca slid his cock further into her mouth, letting her tongue slip down the underside.

Coming slowly up, her hand went up, just brushing her lips. She gently squeezed. When she reached the tip, she twisted back and forth underneath the head. Becca sucked the head harder and more forcefully.

She slipped Joe's dick into her mouth and took him deeper into the warm and wet space. She sucked him in until he touched the back of her throat. He gripped her hair. Becca felt him pulsing against her lips. She moved slowly up and down before releasing him.

Joe pushed her back down to his cock. She licked and sucked the tip. Becca could feel the pent up energy while she worked.

"I have to …" he didn't say anymore.

Becca's nails dug into his flesh. He released into her mouth. She drank his juice readily.

Joe relaxed his grip on Becca's hair. She put his cock away, looked up at him, and licked her lips. Becca looked around and saw the gathering. She stood, handed Joe a business card, turned on her heel, and departed. Joe was left to deal with the crowd. He watched her go. He looked down at the card. "Lady Becca, Dominatrix for Hire," and it listed an email address and phone number.

Poor Little Nikita

Nikita looked up at the sky and watched the slowly fading light. She fidgeted as she waited for her rendezvous. Nervous as Nikita was, the situation made her more so. The person she was waiting for was off-limits during the day, so she could only have him at night. She hadn't figured out why, but that is the way it had to be. It made her sad. She was happy to have him in her life at all. He was an amazing man. Intelligent, funny, and he treated her differently than most people. But he didn't talk to her when he was with his friends. She didn't understand why.

Her breath caught in her throat as she saw him in the twilight at the top of the stairs. His slim frame, dark hair, and clear blue eyes made him look exquisite. She had to remind herself to breathe.

This was her reaction every time he came into a room. She was sure he was aware. He descended the stairs, joining her. They walked in silence until they found a secluded spot. He turned to her.

Nikita sunk to her knees. She wanted to do this. She reached out with trembling fingers. His dick, already hard, strained against the fabric as she unfastened his jeans.

She took his cock out and gently stroked it, her hand cupped his balls. She massaged them lightly as she slid him into her mouth. She took him all the way to the back of her throat. She used short strokes as she moved him in and out. She sucked hard and slow, teasing him.

His hands tangled in her short blonde hair. Her teeth gently slid up his shaft. Her tongue traced circles on the rim of his head. She sucked on it. Her hand followed her mouth as she went pulling him in her moist mouth, then pushing him out with her tongue.

Gently, she squeezed as she went. She could feel his cock pulsing in her mouth. She took him out of her mouth and left him exposed. She pulled her shirt off, revealing her breasts and stomach. She placed a kiss on his cock and stood up. His dick ran through the valley created by her breasts, pressed against her bare skin and fabric of her pants.

"Kiss me just this once so I know what it feels like," she whispered softly, "before I have your cum in my mouth." She saw the conflict in his face.

" Please," she said, "kiss me."

He leaned down and placed his lips on hers.

It was what she had imagined. She pressed harder into him, lips parted as they kissed. Her arms slipped around him. Their tongues danced around each other as they kissed. The passion she felt for him was expressed in that one kiss. Even if he never knew it each time she took him into her mouth. When they broke apart, she slid back down to finish off.

Nikita put his dick in her mouth and buried him in the back of her throat and sucked, moving in short strokes again, leaving him in the back of her throat. Enjoying the pulsing of his vein in her mouth, she felt him start to cum. She drank deeply as he continued, and she never wanted it to end. But it did.

She wiped the corners of her mouth and looked at him with tears in her eyes. She hoped he understood how she really felt and why it hurt her to be ignored.

The Personal Nurse

Janey took a gander at the young man in the bed. He was the only patient in the ward, so it looked like an easy night for her. She was the night shift nurse, and he'd been brought in just as the previous patient was being taken out. That was two hours ago. She observed him and noticed he moved very little. His form was small even though his chart said 5' 10". He was quite handsome. Beautiful was the word that came to mind as she gazed at him. His name was Quinn Rei.

She approached his bed, "Hey honey, I hate to wake you, but I need to take your blood pressure and temp."

A groan and some movement followed.

"I'm Janey, the ward nurse. You happen to be lucky. You're my only patient this evening. You're Quinn, is that right?"

The young man had black hair that was stuck up in various directions.

"Yeah," he replied, squinting up at her.

"Let me dim the light a bit," she said. The light became fifty percent softer, "There. Now I can see your eyes."

Janey stuck a thermometer in his mouth, and a cuff around his arm. She pushed a couple of buttons, and the hum of the inflating cuff was heard. Janey unbuttoned her top a little. Quinn sat up a little. She took off the cuff and took the thermometer, replacing them on the cart.

"So, Quinn, do you want to have a chat? Usually, I'm a personal nurse, but this week I'm filling in for a friend, lucky me."

"Ah, well, I'm never in hospitals so, lucky me that I'm here this week."

Janey had leaned closer. Her bra was now peeking out of her unbuttoned top. Quinn found himself looking there.

"I've worked with a lot of people with a lot of different requests to help them feel better. How about you? Anything I can do for you?"

"I, uhm, like what?"

"Anything."

He reached out and brushed a hand against her breast.

"Even that," she whispered. She dropped the rail on the bed and climbed up on the edge. She wore the old fashioned nurses' uniform that buttoned up. Her shoes fell to the floor with a soft thump. Her hair was pulled back into a ponytail. It was blonde with red streaks in it.

Quinn reached up and unbuttoned the dress the rest of the way. It hung open, revealing a pink lace bra and panty set with matching garters attached to white stockings. He stroked her ample breasts. Her nipples stiffened under his attention. This was the first man she'd been with that was young and not on Viagra.

She leaned forward and pulled the sheet down. She slipped under and straddled him. She let the fabric of her panties rest on his bare cock. The warmth radiated through them. She reached around, unhooked her bra, then uniform and bra came off and hit the floor. They were now in a pile with her shoes.

He grabbed her breasts and took each in his mouth in turn. Janey could feel wetness spreading and his dick getting harder.

"You have no idea how your mouth turns me on," she breathed, "your cock pressing into my pussy is too much."

"Then slip me inside. I want to feel your pussy around my cock."

She pushed the fabric of her panties aside and eased him in. She was a little tight. She began rocking back and forth, sliding up and down.

"Stop. I want to be on top," Quinn said.

Janey helped Quinn rollover. He slipped back inside her and put her legs on his shoulders. He pumped in and out, she moved with him. Her hand wandered to her breasts, and she played with her nipples. Her other hand strayed to her clit. She began stroking when her hips were suddenly tilted up.

She gasped as he rammed harder into her. After several minutes she felt herself getting ready to cum.

"Oh God, oh Quinn, I'm… I'm… make me cum hard."

He respected the request, and she came. She felt him explode inside of her.

"Oh, God," she gasped as she collected all the little orgasms by stimulating her clit.

Quinn was sweating a bit himself. He pulled out and collapsed in the bed next to her.

"Thank you," she whispered to him as he drifted to sleep.

She got up and got dressed. She slipped quietly out and deposited Quinn's chart outside the door.

SHOW 6

Unfinished Business

-For MTF

Lynn was in the lobby. She fidgeted as she checked her watch for the hundredth time. He'd be here soon, and she was nervous. Terrified was more like it. It had been such a long time. The changes in her life … she twisted the silver sapphire ring on her right ring finger. She tried not to think about it.

She found a spot that allowed her a clear view of the lobby doors. She knew she wouldn't be in his direct line of sight. She rechecked her watch. Just a few more minutes. She smoothed the front of her shirt again, and her hands trembled. Her heart thundered in her chest. She took a deep breath and released it slowly to try to calm herself. She failed miserably. Todd was the one that got away. They didn't realize it at the time, both had been too afraid to assert themselves. They had been just teenagers, after all. Sixteen years, one phone call, and one email were far too long.

Lynn deeply regretted that there had been a miscommunication, misunderstanding, and loss. She had attempted many times in the sixteen years to find him. She thought all hope was lost, and one day out of the blue, he found her. Was it fate? Was it Karma? Was it God placing him there? She didn't know, but she didn't want to lose him ever again.

In her musings, she hadn't taken her eyes off the door. She wanted to see Todd first, and her perch was perfect, partially hidden from view. She was going to check her watch when she saw him. He was scanning the room. As she smoothed her purple button-up, she felt the texture of his birthday gift under the cotton fabric. It was a gorgeous black mesh and lace teddy from Victoria's Secret. She took another deep breath and let it out. Here goes nothing.

Lynn stepped out from her hiding spot. He was beautiful. Todd wore a pair of black trousers, a long sleeve dress shirt, and black dress shoes. The shirt was a vibrant shade of cornflower blue; it complemented his stunning blue eyes. She could feel his gaze on her. She smiled. She felt the heat rising up her neck and stop. She was blushing, damn. She hoped that wouldn't happen. Todd dropped his bag as Lynn approached.

She stopped a couple of feet in front of Todd. He hadn't changed a whole lot, besides the gain in height. He had filled out little and wasn't as skinny as he was in high school, but that was fine with Lynn. After all, he had grown up, and he'd grown up quite well.

Lynn couldn't help herself. She had to look into his eyes. After all these years, they still captivated her. She didn't know what to say. It looked like he didn't either. Her gaze never left his face. She was torn on what to do. Kiss him or hug him? She chose the safer route. She wanted to see if the electricity from his touch still ran through her. She lightly touched his arm. Then, she slipped her arms around him in a hug. Todd hugged her back, holding her tightly. She squeezed back and rested her head on his chest. She could hear his heart beating. It was going as fast as hers. That surge of energy poured into her. She knew then that it was okay to let herself go. Her body melted into his. The tingly feelings were still there after all these years. She sighed, and her heart continued to race.

They stood there, in the middle of the lobby, wrapped in each other's embrace for a long time. Neither wanted the moment to end. The pair's hearts calmed down a little, and Lynn looked up at Todd.

"Never wait this long again."

"No. I won't."

They released each other and held hands.

"Where's your bag?" Todd asked as he bent down and retrieved his.

"The concierge was kind enough to keep it for me."

Lynn loved the feel of his hand in hers. His right hand, still strong despite the burns and skin grafts he'd told her about. This was the way it should have been from the beginning. She wouldn't allow herself to go in that direction. She was going to enjoy this time with him.

They approached the check-in, and the concierge looked up. He waved at one of the bellhops. In short order, Lynn had her bags, and they were on their way up to the room. It was on the top floor.

Lynn tried not to let her fear of elevators take over. She held Todd's hand tighter as the elevator lurched upwards. He looked down at her.

"Everything okay?" The corners of his eyes were crinkled, and the corners of his mouth turned down.

"Yeah, elevators are just not my thing," Lynn replied. She looked up at him and smiled a tight smile. He put his arm around her, never letting go of her hand. He held her to him. She felt safer now. It was a quick ride up in the comfort of Todd's arms.

They made it to their suite. Lynn put away her bags and sat on the couch in the living area. Todd sat down next to her. He put his hand on her knee. That little electric jolt went racing up her from the point of his touch.

She put her hand over his and picked it up, then let her shoes drop to the floor as she turned to face him. She sat with one leg tucked up close to her and the other dangling over the edge of the couch; his hand still clutched in hers. Her left knee touched his hip, and her right knee touched his knee. She put his hand on her cheek, closed her eyes, and lightly kissed his palm. She inhaled the scent of his skin, then she opened her eyes and looked at him. Lynn wanted this forever.

They leaned slowly in, and their lips met in a passion fueled kiss. Without breaking the moment, Lynn climbed into Todd's lap, straddling him.

Her hands were on his chest now. His hand had found its way into her golden locks, and had a firm hold. He broke away from her. Using his grip on her hair, he gently pulled her head back, exposing the flesh of her slender neck. He kissed her earlobe and kissed his way down her neck to the top button of her shirt. He pulled her shirt to one side, exposing the top of her breast. Peeking out from the shirt was the lace of the teddy.

Lynn unbuttoned the button and revealed more of the garment. She loved it. She pulled loose from Todd's grasp, then bent forward. She kissed him while she deftly unbuttoned his shirt. She slipped her hands inside the shirt. Lynn gently dug her nails into his skin and slowly dragged them down. She kissed his neck, then his chest. She could feel his excitement through her jeans. Lynn slid lower, kissing his body as she went. She stopped at his waistband, unfastening his pants, and very slowly pulled the zipper down. She pushed the material aside as if she were searching for buried treasure. Lynn achieved her goal, and soon Todd's cock was in her hand.

Lynn licked her lips. She put the tip in her mouth, and her tongue licked it like a lollipop, gently sucking. Lynn gripped the base of his cock. Slowly, she worked her way down, being careful not to nick him with her teeth. Todd's hands were tangled in her hair.

Lynn's head bobbed up and down as she sucked. Her hand applied gentle pressure as it followed her lips up and down his cock. He pushed her head gently, urging her to continue. She could feel him throbbing, but didn't want him to cum yet. She let him go. As she looked into his eyes, she licked her lips again.

Todd untangled his hands and leaned forward. He put his hands on her shoulders and kissed her. She sighed. Todd slid his hands down to her breasts, cupping them. His thumbs caressed her nipples through the fabric.

Lynn's breath caught. He pulled her up, and they stood. He unbuttoned her shirt the rest of the way. When he was done, he peeled it off and left it on the floor next to her. The lace of the teddy had moved to expose her nipples.

Todd bent down and took one his mouth. Lynn placed a hand on the back of his head as he suckled. She could feel the heat growing between her legs.

With her free hand, she unfastened her jeans. She had to have him. Lynn pulled her hand away from Todd's head and shoved her jeans down past her hips.

Todd let go of her breast and looked up at her. One hand slipped behind her back into a half hug. Using his other hand, he slowly dragged his fingertips down her side to her hip, across her lower abdomen to her crotch and the fabric covering her. He caressed the fabric. His eyes never left hers.

"Kiss me again," Lynn whispered.

Todd smiled and obliged. His hand remained in place, still caressing. Their tongues danced in her mouth as they fought to occupy space. Lynn let a small moan escape as she felt the fabric slid aside, and Todd's fingers found the growing wetness of her pussy. He slipped one inside her as if testing the waters.

Lynn couldn't wait. She'd waited long enough for this moment, a moment that should have happened years ago. She squirmed under his touch. Lynn took this opportunity to slide the straps of the teddy down one at a time.

One hand was on Todd's neck as she tugged the mesh and lace down.

"I want you now, please." Lynn looked at him with pleading eyes. Who could say no? He helped her remove the rest of her garments and left them in a pile. She smiled. She led him to the bed.

Lynn playfully shoved him on to it. She got on her knees and, with very deliberate movements, removed his shoes and socks. Then she took hold of the waistband of his pants and tugged. He lifted up enough to allow the passage of the fabric, leaving him half-naked. When Todd had his own pile of clothes next to the bed, Lynn rose from her knees. She pushed him back and lowered herself down onto his waiting cock. Her eyes closed and savored the fit. She never would have imagined that he would be this perfect.

Lynn leaned forward, her muscles tightening around him. Todd put his hands on her hips. Gently, he rolled her over onto her back, so he was standing. Lynn wrapped her legs around his hips as he slipped back into her. She held him there, savoring the feel of his cock inside her. She let him go and was going to let her legs dangle from the bed, but Todd took hold of them. He wrapped them around his waist. With Lynn's hips tilted up, Todd began pumping slowly into her. His eyes never left hers. Lynn's hands were unoccupied, so they began to wander.

They traced invisible lines down her sides, circles on her stomach before resting on her breasts. She caressed them. Todd started thrusting harder, and Lynn's eyes widened as she gasped. She clutched the bedspread and moaned with each thrust. Lynn bit her bottom lip to keep from crying out. She felt the pulsing of Todd's cock as he released into her. He slowly lowered himself on top of her and kissed her. She returned the kiss and wrapped her arms around him. It had been everything she'd anticipated and more.

Todd pulled out and collapsed on the bed next to Lynn. She tilted her head, resting it against his shoulder. She didn't want this moment to end, but it had to. Her stomach growled. The corners of her mouth turned down. She drew in a breath and slowly exhaled.

"I suppose we have to get dressed now?" Todd lifted his head to look down at her.

"Yeah. I haven't eaten today."

Todd propped himself up on his elbow and responded sternly, "Why not?"

Lynn rolled onto her side and mirrored him. "I was entirely too nervous."

"I'm glad I wasn't the only one."

"The phrase butterflies in my stomach? I had elephants instead." Lynn smiled.

Todd slipped his hand onto her waist. "Me too." He leaned over and kissed her. Lynn returned the kiss. She came up off her elbow and gently pushed him onto his back. Her breasts brushed his skin, sending that small jolt of electricity through her again. He cupped her breasts as they kissed passionately. Unfortunately, their moment of renewed passion was interrupted by the complaints of both of their stomachs.

They broke the kiss and grinned at each other. As much as the pair didn't want to, Todd and Lynn removed themselves from the bed. Lynn hung the teddy in the closet. She chose a pair of purple lace panties and a matching bra from her bag. She slowly pulled her panties up, teasing him. Lynn pulled on her jeans in the same slow manner. She left them undone as she pulled on and fastened her bra. Then, she picked up her shirt. Lynn pulled it on and left it hanging open.

Todd watched as Lynn got dressed. She was teasing him, and he was getting hard all over again. The look of her hair as Lynn bent forward was sexy. She looked up at him as she pulled up her panties, and her eyes peeked through the curtain of golden hair. The way her hair traced its way up her leg before settling on her shoulders and gently brushing her breasts as she moved was driving him crazy. He wanted her, and he knew that their time together was short. How could they manage to be apart again?

Lynn looked at Todd and noticed that her deliberate movements had the desired effect. She was hoping to find a little out of the way bistro that she could surprise him in. Lynn wanted to squeeze the last fifteen missed years into these four days. She had missed him, and this was her opportunity to show him how much. She could feel her heart pounding in her chest. Lynn looked at him through her hair, which she now needed to brush. Her heart swelled. She knew this feeling, and she was terrified of what it meant for them.

She'd had several other men move through her life, but until that one message, she hadn't realized just how much she'd… no should couldn't say that word. She missed him; that was certain. She buttoned her shirt just as slowly, lost in thought. She mechanically picked up her hairbrush and began brushing.

Todd got dressed as he continued watching Lynn. He could tell she was deep in thought. After his shoes were on, he stayed her hand with the hairbrush. He cupped her chin, tipped her face up, and looked in her eyes. He kissed her and took the brush. Todd turned her around and slowly ran the brush through her beautiful hair. He knew she'd kept it long just for him. He also knew that she was enduring the weight of it and headaches just for him. That made him … even more conflicted. He had thought of her often over the years, wondering what had happened to her. It was a complete fluke that he'd found her. It was a weird twist of fate or maybe some other cosmic force mocking them. Had they realized all those years ago, they wouldn't be in this situation.

Gentle pressure against his chest brought Todd out of his thoughts. Lynn had leaned into him and rested her head against his shoulder.

"What are we going to do?" She asked softly.

"I don't know." Todd sighed and wrapped his arms around her.

She placed her hands on his arms as they wrapped around her. She took a deep breath, savoring the scent of his skin. She closed her eyes and let the breath go. It came out in a sigh.

"I feel the same way." He placed his forehead against her head.

The tender moment was disrupted by the protests of hunger from their empty stomachs. Lynn couldn't help but laugh.

"We should do something about that first, though."

Todd put down the brush, took her hand, and led her out of the room.

Lynn clung to Todd during the elevator trip. He was enjoying the closeness. He hated that the elevator bothered her this much. And he knew that when they left in a few days that he wouldn't want to go. So he just held Lynn.

Lynn knew that in a few days, this would end. She didn't want to be apart from him again. It would hurt too much, and a hole was being filled. One that she hadn't known existed until he'd found her. There had always been something in the back of her mind. None of her other relationships had filled her heart the way he did. He'd been there the entire time, and she hadn't seen it. He was in her heart, but she didn't want to say it. How could she tell him she loved him? She was afraid of losing him all over again. She didn't know if she could bear it.

The ride down was too short. Lynn and Todd held hands and stepped out to greet the Mississippi afternoon. It was humid despite the cooling temperatures. Todd put his arm around her shoulders. She slipped her arm around his waist, and they strolled down the sidewalk. They ducked into the Horseshoe casino. Lynn spotted a little place she hadn't seen in years, T.J. Cinnamons.

"Let's go there!"

Todd let out a little laugh and replied, "Okay."

Lynn's sadness was lifted by the lighthearted laugh from her … Todd. She pondered what they were now. Were they officially lovers? Were they friends with benefits? They would always be friends, that was certain, but this… something that should have always been?

Todd couldn't stop thinking. This first physical encounter since high school with someone he'd lo- cared deeply for, since then. He was just as confused now as he had been then but for entirely different reasons. Then he'd been a teenager that didn't think she was interested, even after the Sheraton incident. He knew what he was feeling, and they had both made some really deep confessions during their first chat last year. How could they both not notice? How could they both have made the exact same mistake?

They both ordered and were in the midst of a quiet meal. The couple stole glances at the other, hardly believing that they were here together after so long. Lynn blushed each time Todd's gaze met hers. She was sure he could hear her heartbeat.

The table they'd chosen was in a corner away from the door out into the casino. But, the noise was still seeping in. Lynn knew that he'd requested staying at a casino, but she hoped they'd spend time together. She lo- she wanted to bask in his attention. Lynn tried to give him all her attention and flashing lights, clanging glasses, and shouts of disbelief (or joy whatever the case may be) were not conducive to full attention. But she would manage if that's what he wanted to do.

Lynn picked up her napkin, wiped her mouth, and set it aside. She was full, and now she was ready to devote her time to Todd. She studied him. His hair was no longer the blond from all those years ago. Now it was a sandy color. His eyes were still the same blue that had penetrated her heart all those years ago. But now, they seemed a little sad. Perhaps they reflected his internal conflict. His face had filled out when he'd grown up. She'd missed it. She'd missed it all. She was in love with that face. There, she admitted it to herself. She still loved him. That feeling had never gone away. It had just been buried deep in the back of her subconscious.

Todd stared at Lynn. He wanted to know what she was thinking. He'd been right, she hadn't changed a whole lot since high school. She had filled out in all the right places and was even more beautiful. And she was witty and smart. All the reasons he'd fallen for her. Well, he couldn't dwell on all the mistakes they'd made. He was going to make the most of here and now. They would have to deal with whatever consequences came along.

"So, what do you want to do now?" Todd asked.

"Well, I was thinking just walk around for a little while. Have a chat. Sound okay?"

"I think that is manageable. For a little while anyway," Todd replied as his mouth curled into a grin.

Lynn stood and held out her hand to him. He took it, and they were off. They exited the Horseshoe Casino and Resort and continued walking at a leisurely pace. The place was littered with casinos and shops. If there wasn't a casino, there was a shopping experience of some kind.

Lynn had a fleeting thought about what she wanted to do. She kept that idea in the back of her mind.

"So, tell me what you're thinking," she said.

"Ah, well, I was thinking about how awesome it is to be here with you. How much I've missed you. Emailing, talking on the phone, texting … nothing like really being here with you. I think, well, never mind."

"I was thinking the same thing. Having you with me like I wanted all those years ago. It's brought all those feelings back. I was too afraid that you'd not accept me because … well, I thought it would be awkward at family functions. But that's apparently irrelevant."

She brought his hand up and gave it a feathery kiss. He returned the gesture, and there was that jolt. Her heart stopped for a second.

"Do that again," she said.

"Do what?"

Lynn stopped in the middle of the sidewalk. She turned, faced him, and took his hand. Lynn kissed it again. This time she kept her eyes on his. She saw it. Right there in his eyes. He felt it too. That jolt of … longing, need?

"Oh."

One side of Lynn's mouth twisted up into a smirk. "Glad I'm not the only one that felt that."

"So, what are we going to do about it?"

"I don't know. Can I tell you, honestly, what I'm feeling right now?" She asked.

"Sure."

"You promise to be completely honest with me as well?"

Todd nodded.

"My heart is about to explode. It's pounding so hard in my chest, it hasn't stopped since I got here and it's gotten worse since you walked in. Every time you touch me, my heart stops, I can't breathe. I don't know what to do," Lynn paused and stepped closer. "I don't want to lose you, and I'm afraid I will if I tell you what I have to. But I have to know if you feel the same way. Even in the few short hours we've had… do you feel like that?"

Todd's brow furrowed. Lynn knew that look. She'd seen it before, but it had been a long time. He was contemplating his answer.

"I… I've never really been good at expressing myself. But there's something about you. I knew I had to be with you when I saw you. I know what I feel. My heart beats faster, my mind races, I can't concentrate ever since I found you again. But being with you here and now, I can think clearly, I can focus, and it all tells me one thing. But I don't know what to do. I have so much to lose. My family, you. You, I don't ever want to lose again, but I don't know how to do this without someone being hurt."

He pulled her into his arms. They were in their own world as the other tourists flowed by them. Lynn's head was on his chest. She heard it beating strongly and fast. She sighed. She looked up at him, he looked down at her and, almost like they were reading each other's minds, said in unison, "I love you."

A weight seemed to lift from around them. Now, they could enjoy the time they had. They got the elephant in the room out the door.

"There's somewhere we need to find. I brought a few things, but I think we'll need supplies," Lynn said.

"Supplies?"

She looked at him and tilted her head to the side.

"Ooohhhh … Supplies." He laughed again. Lynn had missed that sound. She approved of the tone his voice had taken on. It had been a little higher all those years ago. But she found that she liked this version better. It sounded more … wise instead of the smart ass Todd had been. They let each other go.

Hand in hand, they continued walking in search of the nearest adult store. An hour later, they'd found one. It had been very unassuming. The sign had been very tasteful, like the one Lynn had seen in Germany. The pink awning advertising Eva's in a white script didn't seem too out of place. It wasn't bustling, and then they got a closer look at the window displays. Lingerie covered mannequins with vibrators in hand, some had whips. Lynn could feel her face growing warm. Great, she was blushing.

Todd thought it was a bit funny that Lynn was now the color of a fire truck.

"Should I go in and you wait out here?" he asked.

"No. We'll do this together."

The couple ducked into the store. Darkness had started to fall when they reemerged with a black paper gift bag with bright pink tissue paper sticking out. The sales associate had said the packaging would be discreet. She wasn't kidding!

Instead of the leisurely stroll back, they hailed a cab realizing how far they had actually walked. Lynn was anxious to use their purchases, so the faster they got back to the hotel, the better. Todd's arm was wrapped protectively around her for the cab ride. She loved the feeling of safety from the gesture. It had been a long time since she felt this safe, like nothing in the world, could hurt her. She let her hand rest on his thigh.

After the elevator of torture, Lynn made him wait outside. She opened the bag and pulled out one of the plastic packages. She tore it open and slid the body stocking out. It was black with a black lace top and three-quarter sleeves. She put it on taking care not to snag it. She looked at herself in the mirror and sucked in her stomach. Well, he'd already seen her naked, so she guessed it didn't matter. She rolled her head, attempting to ease the tension that was slowly building there. She took a deep breath, opened the door, and stepped out.

Todd was leaning against the wall waiting for the click of the door. His head was tilted back and rested against the wall. His eyes were closed. He couldn't get the scent of strawberries and champagne out of his mind. Lynn's smell. Her skin was drenched in it, and when they'd made love, the scent was more robust.

He didn't know how he could leave her again. He'd been young and stupid the first time, lacking the confidence to give her the benefit of the doubt. He'd left for basic with these thoughts, and all he'd wanted was run away from his life. A life that he'd hated. Maybe it would have been better had he gotten the courage to tell her how he felt. Maybe they'd have been together. Well, that was then, and this is now. He was going to make up for that lost time. He'd hurt all this time, and now that hurt was starting to mend. He'd thought it had already, but … then he'd found Lynn. He sighed, and it was perfect timing.

Lynn pulled the door open just a little and hung the "Do Not Disturb" sign out. Todd put his hand on the door and gently pushed it open. He stepped in and quickly shut it behind him. He didn't want anyone else to see her in this way. He wanted her all for himself.

Todd turned after securing the locks on the door and found no words for the sight before him. Lynn stood by the couch, black high heels, and a one-piece mesh outfit. The lace-covered her breasts just enough that her nipples peeked out and rested on her shoulders, leaving them bare. Her pale skin was flushed. Words couldn't express just how beautiful she was right at that moment.

Lynn stood by the couch. One leg crossed over the other, trying desperately not to fall over. She hoped that she was at least looking sexy.

She looked at Todd expectantly. The wide eyes and open mouth told her it had the desired effect. Lynn's eyes traveled down Todd's body. She hoped he would come to his senses soon. She was getting cold. She took a step forward.

Todd couldn't believe his eyes. Her hair was hanging in waves down her back. She took a step, and it swung gently behind her. He met her, making only three long strides forward. He grabbed her and pulled her into him, gripping her backside. His right hand slid slowly up to the middle of her back under her hair. He suddenly knew what she meant about the little jolts of electricity when they touched. He felt like he was going to explode.

Lynn returned the sudden embrace. She liked the way his backside felt under her hands. She looked up, and Todd leaned down. Her lips met his in a passion fueled kiss. She poured all of herself into that kiss. Her hands found their way up to his neck, and she leaned into him. He had to have her right now. He couldn't wait. He impatiently tugged at that silly thing she had wanted. But Lynn had asked. It hadn't been very much, and she did say it wouldn't matter if it didn't make it home with her.

He got the lace off and down to her waist. Her full breasts teased him. The paleness of her skin was perfection. Even the German girls could get a little tan happy, and that wasn't sexy to him. Lynn was as hot now as she had been in high school. He kissed the tops of her breasts and slowly trailed kisses down to the fabric of her bodystocking. Todd kissed the cloth covering her pussy. He hooked his fingers over the material that sat on her hips and pulled it down to her ankles. She put her hand on the couch as Todd lifted her leg, one at a time, and slipped her shoes and bodystocking off. He put the heels back on and gently nudged her back to the wall while remaining on his knees.

Lynn was now naked, except for her heels. Todd kissed her inner thighs as she took small steps back. Her skin tingled, and she could feel herself getting wetter. Her back soon touched the wall. Todd caressed her hips and placed one of her legs over his shoulder. He rested his hands on her hips, and he kissed her again.

His tongue flicked out across her clit. He could taste her excitement as he slowly licked her clit. She let out a low moan when he slipped his tongue back and sunk it into her pussy. He licked the inside of her like he was licking an ice cream cone. She cried out and rocked her hips back and forth. Todd pulled his tongue out and sucked her clit hard. She tightened her muscles, and the heel of her shoe dug into his back.

"Todd," she moaned, "I need you inside."

He continued to suck and, with his other hand, pulled down his zipper.

He pulled out his dick, and he gripped her again as he leaned back, pulling her with him. Her foot touched the floor, and Lynn slid it around, so her knees were now on the floor. His face was still buried in her pussy. She pulled away from him and found his waiting dick. She sank down, and he immersed himself into her.

Noel's Tragedy

-For VMcA

His long, slender fingers stroked her stomach like he was gently strumming his guitar. His long body pressed into her bareback, legs intertwined with hers like they had been lovers forever. Noel felt Vin's chest rise with slow, shallow breaths. She didn't know how long it had been since he'd slept like that. She knew that she hadn't ever felt safe enough with anyone to sleep, but here Noel was, her mind slowing and her eyes heavy in the arms of her new lover, a feeling of safety that she'd never felt before.

Noel didn't know how long she'd been asleep when his beard awakened her as he kissed her neck, then her shoulder, and the soft caress of those fingers on her breasts. She shifted, but Vin held her tight against him, and he rolled onto his back and pulled her along with him. She could feel his cock, thick and hard, against her.

She wanted to turn to face him so severely, but he kept her still with one well-developed arm, and his other hand explored her body, meandering to her inner thigh and up to her clit. Vin stroked her, and she arched her back as much as she could despite being pinned down.

Noel stretched her fingers out, searching for his cock, however she couldn't reach it because he'd squeezed harder.

"But babe, I need you," she whispered.

Without a word, Vin released her. Before she could slip him inside, he gently grabbed her arm, pulled her off, and rolled over on top of her. He kissed her. Roughly at first, then more gently. Noel wasn't sure she'd ever get used to kissing him, but it felt nice. Vin's beard tickled her skin as he left a trail of soft kisses down her neck, her breasts, and then her stomach.

He lifted one of her legs onto his shoulder and then the other. Noel could feel his breath, warm and slow against her clit. She watched him and bit her lower lip as his tongue flicked over the sensitive and engorged skin. He watched her as he worked. She studied the almond shape of his brown eyes. She tried to prolong what was coming by concentrating on those beautiful and unique eyes, but she failed, and it wasn't long before she climaxed. Vin didn't stop at the big one. He kept working until she gave him all the little ones, too. She reached for his face. She wanted to know what she tasted like on him.

"Kiss me," she sighed.

Vin pulled away, put her legs down, and slowly slid skin against skin up her body. As she requested, he kissed her. Noel loved how he felt against her, like he was made to be there; she loved that he made her feel desirable. Something she hadn't felt in a very long time. Noel had to return the favor. She bridged, trapped, and collapsed an arm, then rolled him.

She grinned. Her fingers traced lines down Vin's torso, following the trail of kisses she delicately placed down to his cock. Her tongue traced the head before she took him into her warm, wet mouth. She slowly went down. His cock fit perfectly. She gripped the base, gently squeezed, and her hand followed her mouth up, lightly twisting. She did the same on the way back down. She sucked hard. Vin's hands found her hair, and his fingers curled in the waves of blonde. He tugged. She went faster until she could feel him throbbing in her mouth. He pulled out of her mouth and released it on her face.

Dripping with his semen, she looked up at him. He had deprived her of the sweet taste. Vin smirked. She grabbed the edge of the sheet and wiped her face off.

She snuggled up, fitting nicely against him, and lightly ran her fingertips up and down his flank, then ran her fingers through the ginger hair on his chest. Her arm was across his stomach when she kissed him, digging her nails into his flesh. He grunted, broke away from her kiss, and playfully frowned. She smirked back.

He pushed her away, but that wouldn't deter her. She wanted Vin inside her in the worst way. She could feel the wetness from her pussy as she ached for his dick. He started to turn his back when she grabbed his arm, forcing him onto his back. She threw a leg over him and leaned forward, her forehead touching his.

"I. Want. You. Inside. Me."

Vin grabbed her breasts roughly before he suckled each one. His beard tickled her skin again. He stretched up and whispered into her ear, "Only if you're on your knees."

Noel climbed off and went to all fours. He scooted around behind her, shifted her to the center of the bed, and entered her from behind. She dropped to her forearms and pushed her hips up. He felt so good filling her. She couldn't concentrate to stroke her clit as he moved in and out. Her breath caught in her throat as she felt the pressure building.

"God, fuck me harder," she gasped.

He complied. Noel could feel herself cumming, and Vin slowed.

"Nooo," she moaned, "Don't stop."

His thrusts slowed; Vin leaned forward and grabbed a breast. He rolled her nipple between his fingers. That hand went up to her neck and into her hair. He grabbed a fistful and gently pulled her head back. He thrust faster.

Noel moaned low. The pressure was building again. She felt herself cumming. Again. This time she felt him throbbing in her pussy. He slowed again, and he was deep inside her as he released.

Vin pulled out and collapsed beside her. She rolled to face him. She placed a hand on his cheek and stroked his beard before kissing him. Noel snuggled into his chest. He wrapped his arms around her, and they drifted off to sleep.

Noel shifted in the bed, rolled over, and cracked an eye. Light streamed through the window. She smiled, felt the space where he'd been, and realized she was at home in her bed. It had been a wonderfully cruel dream. Her heart broke. She checked her phone, and there was nothing. She cursed herself for being vocal about her feelings and was confident that her dream would never come true.

A truck rumbled to a stop outside. Noel lifted the blinds, and it was UPS. She couldn't imagine what it was. Noel couldn't recall anything that she'd ordered. A large box with a smaller one stacked on top emerged with only legs and fingertips visible.

Noel dropped the blind and threw on her red satin robe. She dashed down the stairs and threw open the door as the driver set the boxes down.

"If you would," he offered her the tablet.

She signed for it and shoved the boxes inside. She secured the door and looked at the labels. Indeed they were addressed to her. She looked at the return address and squealed. It didn't take her long to pop the boxes and get the contents up to her room. She would have to make room but later. Her Esse Liberator lounge would just have to take up space in the middle of the room.

Noel got it up, and together just as there was a knock on the door. She peered through the blinds again. It was a vehicle Noel vaguely recognized from a picture someone had posted on Snapchat. She flew down the stairs again and tore open the door. He was standing there. She grabbed Vin and pulled him inside.

She locked the door, and without any hesitation, she kissed him, despite being unsure how he would react as this was the first time they had met in person. Vin returned her kiss with equal fire. When they came up for air, Noel studied him. She took his hand and led him up to her room.

She pushed the lounge forward and turned to Vin. He shut the door. Noel sat on the purple covered lounge, her robe falling open. She reached for Vin and pulled him to her. Noel unfastened his shorts, shoved them down, and discovered he was ready for her. She took his cock into her mouth, and it was better than her dream.

Noel moved him in and out of her mouth, her tongue teasing the tip as she gently sucked before taking his shaft in all the way. Her right hand gripped the base and followed her lips up, squeezing as she rotated. Her other hand grabbed his ass. Vin's hand found her hair. He shoved hard, fucking her mouth as she sucked. She felt the throbbing on her lips and under her hand. He tried pulling her away, but she dug her nails into his skin and forced him to cum in her mouth. She drank it down as if her life depended on it.

Vin pulled out when he finished. Noel daintily dabbed at the corners of her mouth; a smirk played there.

He pushed her back onto the lounge. She arranged the pillows as he pulled his shirt off. When she turned around, she gasped, and her eyes went wide. He was magnificent, even better than the picture he'd posted. What had she expected? She hadn't, and she was never this lucky. She reached for him, but he pulled the tie from her robe and hooked her up.

Noel raised her now bound hands above her head, resting them on the pillow.

"Babe, I need you," she wailed.

Vin pushed the robe all the way open. He leaned over and massaged her breasts before sucking them. He slipped a slender finger inside her and then slid his thick dick inside.

Noel sighed. He pulled her backside to the edge of the lounge and continued to thrust. He watched her face. She bit her lip.

"Don't hold back; we're alone," he ordered, his voice huskier than usual.

Noel moaned, "Harder, baby."

The sound of skin slapping skin rose above her quiet grunts of pleasure. Vin smirked as she sucked in air. He pulled out and grabbed her legs. Vin flipped her over, and she was helpless to stop him. He entered her from behind, doggy-style. This position was not her favorite, but she'd already cum once, and she knew that he knew it. She pushed her hips up and back into him, allowing Vin deeper penetration, and she gasped again. How was it that he could make her do that?

"Faster!" she moaned.

He squeezed her hips as he thrust faster. She felt the pressure building again for the - she didn't know how many times... Noel could hardly stand it as she felt him throbbing inside her. One last hard thrust, and Vin let go. She could feel it; she loved how it felt. She hadn't had that in such a long time, and he was perfect.

Vin pulled out. Noel presented him with her bound hands. He released her, and she handed him a towel.

She moved to her bed, and he followed. They laid together, despite the small size, and it was like her dream. He fit like they had been lovers forever. His strong arms around her, and she finally felt safe and finally felt loved again.

Noel stirred and rolled over. She was alone again, her bed cold. The lounge, gone with no evidence it had ever been there.

"Fuck my life," she sighed as she realized it was a dream within a dream. She got out of bed, grabbed her cell, and hit the shower. Maybe he would show, perhaps he wouldn't. She'd be scrubbed up and dressed, just in case.

Noel popped her phone in the holder in the shower before starting the water. She looked at herself in the mirror. All the self-doubt and miserable feelings Noel ever had about herself spilled out down her cheeks. She wiped them away with the back of her hand. What was wrong with her? At her age, she should be confident in herself, but she doubted that he wanted her. She couldn't believe her luck when she found him on that stupid dating app. But after three months of chatting, he'd made her feel again. He made her remember all the things that she wanted to try, not just in life but in the bedroom. She could write about it all day but to experience it. True, it required trust, and she was willing to put that trust in Vin because something about him made her trust. She didn't have alarm bells going off in her head like that last one.

She shook her head to clear the negativity, then climbed in the shower and let the water cascade over her. Noel turned on her Spotify favorites playlist, and the first song that floated out of the tiny phone speaker was one that Vin had sent her almost two months ago. She leaned against the wall and took a deep breath. Noel let the water run until the song finished, then switched the showerhead to massage. She stood with her back to the water. Noel reached out of the shower curtain and brought a knife in. She opened Snapchat, flipped open their chat, and held down the snap button.

Noel looked right in the camera.

"I loved you, and I'm sorry that I was not enough or what you wanted."

On the outstretched arm, she pressed down and drew the blade across her arm.

She released the button and tapped send. She leaned against the wall, slid down into the tub as the water pounded on her. Her blood slowly leaked out. The knife clattered down into the tub, but the door flew open, and the curtain flew back. Vin grabbed her towel from the hook, turned the water off, and scooped her up. He cradled her in his thick arms, carrying her to the bedroom.

"I was on my way, sexy mama. I'm so sorry I got held up. You are enough."

Vin laid her on the bed, putting the towel under her arm to soak up the blood while he found a suitable dressing. He returned with gauze and tape. He dressed the cut and put the items aside, then took her hands. His eyes scanned her nakedness. He sighed. Vin tried to look her in the eyes before he spoke.

"You're impossible."

Noel looked up at him.

"I can't believe you're finally in my bedroom. What took you so long?"

"Stupidity, confusion. I don't know."

Noel opened her mouth to say something, but Vin kissed her. His tongue found its way to hers. Her arms slipped around his neck. He put his hands on her waist, slid one up to a breast which he caressed, and then kneaded. She moaned as his thumb brushed her nipple. She placed her hand on his in an attempt to direct his fingers to repeat that action.

"You like that?" he breathed.

"Yeah," Noel sighed. "Do it again."

"Not yet," he responded.

Vin kissed her jawline, then her neck until he got to the curve. He traced the area with his tongue as if he were looking for just the right spot. He sucked, hard leaving his mark before he nipped her. Noel gasped and dug her fingernails into his neck. She felt him grin against her skin. He bit her harder, pulling her flesh with his teeth. She pressed against him, her other hand found its way to his hair, and she gently pushed his head into the crook of her neck.

"Again and harder, baby," she pleaded.

He pushed back against her hand. Vin's eyes sought hers. She saw only mischief there. She would not get him to do anything she asked. He was exerting his wills, and his wants to see how she reacted since this was the first time they had been together.

"I'll come back to that if you're a good girl."

"Mmhmm."

Vin left his hand on her breast and roughly grabbed the other. He sucked her hard. So hard that Noel pressed against him, trying to fight the orgasm that was coming, but she failed and whimpered as her body convulsed under his. His hand left her breast, traced a light trail down her side to her ass. Vin gripped it, digging his nails into her flesh. Then, he pulled her leg up and spanked her.

"Again, baby," Noel gasped.

This Vin did readily. He spanked her again and again as he sucked her breast. Noel orgasmed again before Vin released her raw nipple.

"That's a good girl," he smirked.

Noel was a quivering mess. Vin pulled off his shirt and unfastened his pants, whipping out his short, thick cock. He got on his knees on the bed, grabbed a pillow, folded it in half, and stuffed it under Noel's backside. He put her legs up on his shoulders and slipped inside her hot, dripping pussy.

Noel gasped as she felt the thick cock inside her. She'd never had a man as thick as he was inside her. He filled her up better than any of her previous lovers, and she'd had a few. Vin's hands were on her hips as he thrust inside her.

"Turn over," he demanded.

She pulled her legs down and flipped on her stomach, then on all fours. She put her breasts on the bed. Her was up ass in the air, ready for Vin. He grabbed her hips, spread her legs a little wider, and sunk into her. She could feel him hitting her g-spot just enough that she was going to cum. She could feel it. She reached through and stroked her clit. She had to get off and cum; she couldn't have just one and not the other. That was cruel.

"You're so tight. Such a good girl, saving this pussy for me," Vin moaned as he thrust.

Noel pushed her hips back into him.

"Baby, I'm gonna cum," she cried.

"Me too," he responded as he started to pull out.

"Cum inside me. I want you to feel me up," she pleaded.

Vin left his cock, throbbing inside her as he expelled his hot white cum.

"Oh God," she cried as she released.

Vin spanked her.

"Again, baby."

He obliged. Then, he pulled out. Noel looked over her shoulder. She wiggled around, licked his cock clean; then she slipped it in her mouth and sucked. Noel's tongue caressed him. His hands wound up tangled in her hair. He gripped her tightly and shoved his cock as far as it would go, fucking her mouth. Noel's hands caressed his ass. When he started to go hard in her mouth, she dug her nails into his skin, and he went harder. She pulled back and let him slip out of her mouth. She could only take so much of a mouth fuck, especially with the girth of his cock, before her jaw would lock.

Noel pressed against Vin as she slid herself up against his body. When she got up enough to look him in the eye, she whispered.

"My turn."

"Oh yeah?" he grunted.

"Yeah."

She reached for her handcuffs, which were in her goody bag beside the bed. She slapped them on Vin, and he grinned.

"I didn't think you had this in you," he snarked.

Noel grabbed his shoulder, turned him, and shoved Vin back on the bed. She reached into the bag again, this time to retrieve a leather strap. She lifted Vin's arms. Then she fastened the chain of the cuffs to the rail of the headboard with the strap. She grinned. She reached again, extracting two pieces of cloth. One covered Vin's eyes, the other… she fashioned a gag and well, gagged him. He struggled against them a little until Noel caressed his beard.

"You've got to learn patience, baby."

She kissed his chest, teased his nipples with her tongue, and rubbed his cock. She shimmied his shorts off and was pleasantly surprised that he was sans hair. Noel stroked his balls, fondling them as she sucked his cock like a candy cane. When she felt him pulsing in her mouth, she stopped, teasing the tip with her tongue. Noel pressed against him again as she went up his body, her nipples erect from the friction. She was ready now, too. She straddled him and slipped his soup can cock into her pussy.

Noel leaned forward, rocking her hips and going slightly up and down. She could feel the pressure against her clit, and it was terrific. His cock inside her was amazing, and he was a good sport letting her bind him up. She bounced up and down, her breasts dancing, and Vin moaned through the gag.

Noel slowed and leaned forward enough to let her nipples graze his skin.

"What's that, baby? Do you want me to take off your gag and blindfold?"

Vin nodded.

"Will you finish letting me fuck you this way?" Noel inquired.

Vin nodded.

She took the gag and blindfold off without leaving her perch and his cock.

"I want to see those tits bounce," he demanded.

"As you wish," she replied.

Noel figure-eighted her hips before resuming her leaned forward up and down bounce. Vin watched, mesmerized by Noel's sizeable breasts bouncing.

"I need to hold them. Suck them," Vin whimpered.

Noel slowly leaned forward, releasing Vin's cock from the warmth of her pussy, and stretched out, dangling her breasts in his face. He leaned up and latched onto the one he hadn't sucked before, causing Noel to gasp. She pulled back, Vin tried to come with her, but the restraints held him back.

She slipped his cock back inside and continued her labors until they both came. In Noel's case, she repeatedly orgasmed as she rocked back and forth against Vin while he emptied into her. When Noel was sure he was finished, she collapsed onto him. She reached over to her CD stand and fumbled for the key. Once her fingers curled around it, she released Vin. His wrists were already starting to bruise.

Vin wrapped his arms around her. He kissed the top of her head.

"No one has ever had the guts to do that to me. Now, I kinda understand," he said, his voice thick with sleep.

"Shh, you're safe here," Noel whispered. She snuggled against him, and they both dozed off.

The Loan Shark

Charlotte felt so ... dirty. Work, it always made her feel terrible. She took two showers she felt so horrible. But the money, oh the money was damn good. It almost made up for it. It helped remodel her house, including the shower in her bathroom with one of those excellent top-of-the-line massaging showerheads, handrails, and a bench at just the right spot. The installer had thought she was crazy. He discovered later when they tested it that she wasn't all that crazy when they fucked under the steaming water.

She couldn't explain the fascination with the cold tile and warm water functioning as a sanctuary, or why it was her favorite place to have sex with strangers. Perhaps it was the fact that she felt like she screwed people over all day when they came to her looking for money, and she gave it to them with interest rates so high they would be in debt for years to come. It made her feel ... slimy.

Charlotte reached in and turned the knobs and let the water run. She looked at herself in the mirror. She imagined layers of invisible grime on her clothes as she unbuttoned her shirt and peeled it away, exposing the powder pink colored satin Amelea from Agent Provocateur. It looked bright against her pale skin. She dropped her shirt into the open hamper. She slowly unzipped her pants at the side and slid them down. A matching Amelea thong pressed softly against her smooth flesh. She examined herself again.

She traced the edges of the bra, imagining that her fingers were that of a lover. She was in between at the moment. She slid her fingers over the slippery fabric of the bra. It was just thin enough to feel her nipples beginning to stiffen at her own touch. Sometimes you didn't need a man. She pulled her fingers slowly down between her cleavage, down her abdomen, and to the edge of her panties.

Charlotte hooked one finger around and gently tugged while the other hand found its way to the thick thatch of hair between her legs. She slipped a finger into her vagina, knowing she would find that she was already wet. Charlotte pulled her finger out and stepped to the shower. She turned on the shower and adjusted the head to massage. Charlotte stepped in bra and panties still on. She let the water pound her nipples, and she stretched. She unhooked her bra, slipped it off, and tossed it out onto the floor.

She grabbed her washcloth. She lathered it up and slowly worked it across her torso. She stiffened as she scrubbed her already swollen nipples. Charlotte gently massaged them with her thumbs and pressed against the shower wall, dropping the cloth. She rolled them between her thumb and forefinger, pressing harder and tugging. Charlotte could feel the wetness growing on her panties that was more than the running water. She rolled them off and tossed them out. They landed with a wet splat. She picked up the cloth and continued the methodical scrubbing of her body. She sat on the bench, thinking maybe she should have brought her toy. She sat back and let the shower pound into her flesh again.

Charlotte stood reminding herself she didn't need a man or man parts no matter how much fun a good cock, real or fake, felt inside her. She could get off on her own, and that's exactly what she needed. She took the cloth and massaged her breasts and nipples again to regain the momentum she had. It didn't take long. Once again, she stood and let the shower head work its magic pounding mercilessly into her breasts and nipples, stimulating her even more than her own hands ever could. She slid her hands down and separated her lips, locating her swollen and throbbing clit. She stepped back just enough that a jet of massaging water pulsated on the sensitive flesh causing her breath to catch. She grabbed one of the strategically placed hand bars and willed herself to stay still to get all the little orgasms she could out of this.

She moaned and cried out as she climaxed; she shuddered as she captured all the little ones. She sank to her knees, but she knew she wasn't entirely done yet; there was more to come for her. She lay back on the floor of the spacious shower, and oh, who was she kidding? She had to have a cock. Luck would have it that she had her spare in the plastic toy box under the bench. She whipped out a purple silicon dildo and slid it in her pussy. One hand cupped a breast, working her nipple while the other worked the dildo. The water pulsated and pounded on her clit, and she climaxed again and again. She sighed a huge sigh and relaxed. She knew then she would sleep well tonight.

Just as soon as she uploaded this video to her website.

Car Thief

Gina pulled herself from under the dash as the car roared to life. She grinned. Paxton looked at her.

"Dear God, I had no idea you could do that."

His eyes were wide, and he bit his lip as if he had more to say.

Gina buckled her seatbelt, motioned for Paxton to do the same, dropped the e-brake, pushed in the clutch and shifted, chirping the tires a little as they pulled away. She threw the stick quickly through the gears as they picked up speed, evident that she was a practiced hand at this. She felt the grin spread of its own accord on her face as they entered the interstate. The car, lucky for them, had a full tank of gas. The 1990s Firebird was her dream car. She had owned one once and knew exactly where the weakness in the security system to exploit was. She knew how fast it was and knew that this young piece of man meat in the seat next to her would be impressed with how it handled since he'd been just a baby when it was produced.

"You are good."

"My hobbies include boosting cars and race car driving."

Gina responded and afforded him a glance and a grin. She kept her eyes on the road. There was a turn off she was looking for that led to an empty parking lot where she took all of her conque-- uh, dates. No, conquests was the right word. She had a thing about commitment.

"What are your other hobbies?"

"Oh, men. Sex, guns."

To emphasize her point, Gina took her hand off the stick and placed it on his thigh and slowly slid it to his stick, which, to her delight, was quite hard. She let her hand linger for a moment before sliding it back and to the knob to downshift and catch her exit.

"Where are we going?"

"Pax, I know this place. Quiet, very secluded, where I can drive your stick, or you can park your car in my garage if you'd rather."

"I'll shut up. Just drive."

"I thought you'd say that."

Gina unbuttoned a couple buttons on her shirt to give Paxton a preview while they were driving, and her Agent Provocateur Fifi bra peeked out at him. He tried not to be noticeable.

"You can look. I wouldn't have invited you if I didn't want you to stare."

Paxton unabashedly stared at the fancy black lace. He reached over and slipped his hand inside her shirt to touch it. His hand lingered, and he used his thumb to caress her. She turned into the lot and drove to a back corner. She pulled the e-brake and left the car running.

Gina crawled over the middle console, hiked up her skirt and straddled his thighs, reaching down and kicking the seatback. His hands worked quickly to get her top undone. She had his cock out and in her hands before he'd finished fumbling. She slipped down on top of him, his cock fit inside nicely. She pivoted her hips in slow circular motions. His mouth found her breasts, and he sucked through the fabric. She moaned.

"We need to flip. I want you deeper inside."

"How?"

"Grab me like you're hugging me and roll."

He did as instructed, and awkwardly they switched. Gina kicked off her heels, got situated, propped her feet up on the dash and let Paxton thrust for all he was worth. He put his hands under her backside and helped left her hips more.

"Oh my God," Gina whispered and moaned.

Paxton thrust harder.

"Deeper."

Paxton buried himself into her pussy as far he could go and used short, fast strokes.

"I'm gonna cum," he cried.

"Cum in me, and don't pull out."

Gina slipped her hand down to her swollen clit. She was almost there. Gina rubbed and rubbed as she tightened her muscles and felt Paxton climaxing inside her. She cried out as she released.

He collapsed on top of her with his cock still inside. She kissed his neck.

"Want to do this again tomorrow night?"

Tickets

Casey was late. Holy shit was she ever late. Her first day at the studio and she was fucking late. How could she have overslept? She was speeding down the deserted road. She knew better, but she was in a hurry. She put her Jeep down the road at a surprising speed. But she didn't see the cop that was sitting there waiting for his day to be broken up by the wayward speeder.

Casey didn't see him until he was behind her with his lights flashing. She pulled over and reached for her license and registration — Son of a bitch. A ticket was not what she needed right now. Casey looked at her watch. Oh, she was so fired, and she would never work in film again. There went film school. Fuck. Her head rested against the steering wheel; she was trying not to cry when there was a tap on her window. She raised her head, and she couldn't believe her eyes.

Standing at the window was Zev Jackson. She rolled down the window, turned and looked at him. He hadn't changed a whole lot, just filled out a bit and it looked delicious on him. She doubted that he would recognize her at all. She had lost her baby fat and toned up after a lot of hard work trying to fit in with the kids at film school. Casey noticed Zev was taller than when they were in school.

"Ma'am, are you aware of how fast you were going?"

"Why, yes, Zev, I was aware, but I'm late for work. It's my first day, and I can't be late, but I am."

The officer tilts his hat back leans down, looks at the face staring back at him.

"Casey Howard?"

"Yes."

"What are you doing here?"

"I was speeding. I wanted to meet the handsome cop in the car, and here you are. Who knew it was you and who knew I was right?"

"This is ridiculous. Step out so I can see you. It's been what, ten years?"

"Try fifteen. You skipped the reunion."

Casey opened the door and swung her toned legs around.

"Still drive barefoot. You know that's illegal, right?"

She slid out and planted her feet but not before she lost her balance. Zev caught her. She looked up, he looked down and wow. Casey could feel every inch of her skin tingle just like it did in high school when he would walk by her. Damn. She could feel the tingling reaching to her clit and swiftly working its way to the rest of her vagina. She was starting to get hot and bothered. He leaned down, and she stretched up, their lips meeting in a kiss. Casey, being the strong spirited woman she was, pressed into him and opened her mouth, her tongue snaking out searching for Zev's. She found him quite receptive to her advance. Casey slipped her arms around his neck, and he put a hand on her back and around her waist, pulling her closer. She could feel him through the thick fabric of his pants.

When they finally pulled apart, Casey pressed her lips together, and she closed her eyes. She wanted to savor every second of that kiss and the feel of him against her. Casey imagined what it would be like to have him all the way inside her unlike what had happened all those years ago at that party. She pushed that memory away and looked Zev in the eye.

"I have been waiting for that for so very long."

"Me too."

"What the hell happened?"

Zev leaned down and kissed her again with more passion than the first kiss now that the nerves were out of the way. It was convenient that this was a seldom traveled stretch of road and what a coincidence that he'd been patrolling here today. He wasn't going to miss his chance again. He pulled back.

"Stupidity happened. I didn't see all the little things. I was angry about God only knows what and didn't see the best thing was right in front of me."

"Kiss me again, just like you did. That should have been our first kiss."

Zev kissed her again, and Casey knew that they had to finish what started so long ago. She pulled back, just enough that her face was still inches from Zev's.

"How long you got Officer? The back of the car is pretty roomy, and I'm already late, better make it worth it."

"I may have some time."

Casey removed her hands from Zev, but before she could open the back door, he stopped her.

Zev led her around to the other side of her car.

Casey grabbed his shirt and pulled him to her. She didn't want to let him get away again. His arms encircled her, and they kissed. Casey's hands wandered, finding his zipper and his growing cock underneath. She pulled the zipper down and slipped her fingers in to caress the fabric of his boxer briefs. She left her hand gently stroking him.

Zev pulled his head away, slid his hands down to the hem of her skirt and slipped it up. He was surprised to see that she wore nothing under it.

"Nice."

Casey slipped Zev's hearty cock out.

"You're not so bad yourself, Officer."

Casey leaned against the car as Zev ran a hand down her thigh and placed her leg around his waist as he entered her. Casey shifted, and Zev moved in and out thrusting hard despite the awkward position. She gripped Zev's arms, and she arched her back, tilting her hips and squeezing Zev's cock.

Zev bent his head down and nipped Casey's neck, and she moaned.

"Jesus, do that again."

Zev obliged, this time he slowed his pace and traced a small circle with his tongue before gently biting her.

"Fuck me hard, Zev."

He put one hand on the side of the car and pumped into her as hard as he could. She tightened her muscles down and arched a little more. It had been so long since the last time she came, but she could feel herself climaxing. Zev slowed and came with little more than a grunt. He pressed against her, both breathed heavily.

Zev pulled out of her, Casey relaxed and pulled her skirt down.

"Oh, let me clean that up for you, Officer."

Casey grabbed Zev by the hips and guided him around, so his back was against the car. She sank to her knees and took his cock into her mouth, all the way to the base. Casey sucked. She slid him in and out of her mouth, one hand following her mouth up his shaft, gripping and twisting until he exploded into her mouth and she drank it down. She looked up at him and licked her lips.

"Oh my God."

Casey put his cock away and stood up. She kissed him.

"Am I free to go, Officer?"

"Yes. Call me."

Casey brushed off her knees and walked around to the driver's side. She got in, started the car and pulled away.

Zev got back in his patrol car.

"Shit."

He pulled out a small flat plastic container. He reached around the side of the box on the dash and retrieved the SD card and installed a new one. He put the old one in his pocket for later viewing.

The Warrior and the God

Sadie found herself in the library after midnight. It was exam week, and usually, the place was packed but not tonight. She was one of ten people in the Greek mythology course, so she expected to see her classmates huddled in the corners conducting some last-minute research on the questions from their practice exams. But they weren't. She checked the date on her watch just to be sure that she wasn't off a day. She wasn't. She found a secluded table in a darkish corner and set her bag down.

She unloaded her books and hit the mythology aisle to pull more books. Flyers stuck out from in between the books, so she yanked one out. And that was why the library was devoid of students. One of the frat houses was having an end of exams party, ladies free, and one dollar cover for the guys. Free entry for ladies was kind of standard, but that cover was not. Typically, frat parties were a five dollar cover, not that Sadie would know because she never went. These flyers littered the ground the morning after, and it annoyed her. That's what you get for going to college at thirty rather than right out of high school. She sighed and returned with the other books.

Sadie was knee-deep in a book about Zeus and his strange relationship with Hera when she heard someone clear their throat. She looked up. A slender young man stood there, a book in his hand.

"May I help you?" Sadie inquired politely. He was adorable. Lightly bronzed skin, blue eyes, sun-bleached hair. She could stare at him all day.

"It's more about how I can help you," he smirked.

What the hell was that about? She was kind of curious. What random college-aged guy would skulk around the library when his peers were out partying it up and celebrating freedom until fall.

"How can you help me?"

He approached the table and set the book down.

"I've seen you around the mythology section all semester. I thought you might need this. I tracked it down. One of your classmates had it, so I had a chat with her. It seems she wanted to knock you down a peg and hopes you fail your exam."

"That's… nice of her." Sadie knew who it was, too. The girl was in class only because the professor was eye candy, and she thought it would be an easy A. Tough luck for her.

"Oh, I'm Jason, by the way," he stuck his hand out.

"Sadie," she responded and shook Jason's hand. His grip dismissed any notion that he was as weak as he looked. "Like Jason and the Argonauts?" She paused. "I'm sorry. Can you see where my brain is?"

Jason chuckled, and Sadie could have sworn she saw his eyes twinkle mischievously. He took her other hand and pulled her up.

"Sadie, what would you do if I said I am that very Jason?"

She looked into those twinkling eyes and thought that couldn't be true. Myths were often based on fact, but these myths were thousands of years old.

"I know what you're thinking… I'm thousands of years old and dead. You're almost right. I am older, a lot older, and not dead; once I completed my tasks, I was awarded a couple of gifts, immortality, and time travel."

"Why time travel?" Sadie blurted.

"Why not? Once the gods bestowed immortality on me, it opened my mind up to different thinking. They knew their time was almost over, so they let me travel as I wished. I think they really wanted me to settle down, but I wanted more from my life."

"Let me guess, hard to settle after a life of excitement."

"How did you know?"

"A warrior knows a warrior," Sadie responded.

"You're a warrior?" Jason replied.

"Yes, I was a warrior." Sadie let go of his hands, pulled out her phone, and found a picture of her in uniform with a lot of her Army buddies. She held the phone up.

Jason took the phone, examining the picture. He zoomed in. His eyes looked from the screen to Sadie and back again before he handed it back and, without hesitation, kissed her. Sadie dropped the phone onto the table. She wrapped her arms around him, and he responded in kind, pulling her tight against him. Someone somewhere in the library coughed, and the sound carried, breaking them apart.

"Wow," Sadie breathed.

"Wow, indeed. What were you doing in that picture?"

"Uhm, we had just finished test firing our firearms in Kuwait."

"I've known women that called themselves warriors, and I've known women, but none made me feel like that."

"I've got more pictures if you want to see them."

"Why? I have the warrior in them right in front of me."

Sadie didn't wait for Jason to make the next move. She kissed him, shoving him back toward the table, but he pulled away.

"Am I –" she started.

"Books make the worst sounds when they're shoved to the floor in the silence of a library," he interrupted.

Sadie smirked, and they hastily moved the books to the floor. As soon as Jason stood up, she playfully pushed him onto the table. He pulled Sadie close. Jason ran a hand through her hair, down her neck, and to the collar of her shirt. He lightly ran his fingertips down over her breast, teasing her nipple with his thumb. His other hand gripped her waist.

Sadie bit the inside of her lip. She tugged at the hem of his t-shirt before stripping it off him. She traced his scars. She knew a lot about injuries, each one told a story, and each story was unique to the owner. She thought scars were sexy, especially when they were on warriors. She kissed each scar, working her way down. He stopped her, slid off the table, and lifted her up onto it.

"Fair's fair." He smiled at her and pulled off her shirt.

All Sadie could think was it was a great day to not wear a cute bra and panty set. But she didn't know if that bothered Jason at all. He caressed her breasts, then pulled off her pants before unfastening his own. He paused to trace the white lines of Sadie's scars down her thigh. He squatted and slowly rose, hooking her legs over his shoulders as he came up. His hand found her pussy and slipped a finger in.

Agonizingly slow, Sadie thought. She reached for him.

"Fuck me," she insisted.

He withdrew his finger and buried his cock inside her. He gripped her waist, and she gripped the edges of the table. She let him have control of the situation. He started with slow strokes in and out, in and out. Then a little faster. Sadie squeezed, Jason went faster. Sadie squeezed more. The muscles in her calves ached, and her toes curled, she bit her lip to keep from crying out as she came. Jason slowed. She could feel his cock, still hard inside her. Sadie let go of the table and caressed her breasts. She could feel herself, ready to go again.

"Harder," she whispered.

She felt his pelvis slam into hers as Jason thrust hard and fast. Sweat trickled down his bare chest. Sadie tilted her hips up, engaging her core, to stay in that position, and squeezed her pelvic floor muscles tight. She felt his cock pulsate as he came inside her. He slowed, and she lowered herself to the table. He withdrew his dripping cock. She grabbed her shirt and cleaned him up.

"I have a spare in my bag," she responded to his horrified look. She pulled the back-up shirt out and slipped it on and tossed the sperm-filled one inside. She tucked him back in his pants, handed him his shirt, then pulled on her own pants.

"Aren't you worried –"

"About what?" she asked.

"Getting pregnant?"

"Well, I've been told that getting pregnant may be more difficult or never happen. Injury from the war," Sadie replied.

"So, you –"

"Do this often? No. First time, but something told me that you were the right one."

Jason smiled at her. He took her hand and pulled her close.

"I want my warrior to pass her exam and then travel with me," his voice had grown husky, "I want to make love to you forever."

Sadie kissed him. "Come back to my place, and we can discuss it."

Jason let her pull away from his grasp and assisted in the cleanup of the book mess she'd made. Sadie hefted her bag onto her shoulder, but Jason took it, threw the strap over his head, and settled it across his chest.

"I know you're a warrior and probably used to doing his yourself, but I am honored to carry your burden," he said with a bow.

She pulled him out of his bow and kissed him again, this time wrapping her arms around him. Jason wrapped her up as well, and the world dissolved around them.

SHOW 12

Vanilla

-Written by Jemma Bixby

Cam approached her, his eyes on her lips. He readied himself for their feel, their taste - how he had imagined it. He hadn't even touched her yet, but he was already hard. Cam reached out and took her arms, his thumbs caressing the flesh underneath. Smiling, Jill leaned back against the post and tilted her head upward in anticipation of his mouth on hers. But Cam decided to go another way. He leaned in and kissed the hollow of her throat first then trailed his lips upward on her neck, kissing her jawline. Cam made his way up to her earlobe and took it between his teeth. His hot breath tickled her ear, and she wriggled against him. Jill moaned and arched her body against his. He put one hand on her waist and pulled her closer to him. The feel of her breasts against him drove him mad, making him want to rip her clothes off right then and there. But with this woman, he was going to take his time, tease her until she begged him to make her cum.

He finally crushed his lips against hers; she made a little sound in the back of her throat, a plea for gratification. Cam kept his kisses gentle and soft and moved his lips in small circles on hers, only giving her a full kiss every couple of seconds. Jill hugged him tighter and dug her fingers in his back. He smiled. Her need for him was already starting to overwhelm her. We have a long way to go, gorgeous, he thought to himself. Be patient.

Cam's own body stiffened as he restrained himself. He cupped her jaw, pulling her face closer so he could kiss her deeper. Jill's breathing intensified, and she whimpered.

He slid one hand up to the base of her neck and wrapped his fingers in her hair. The other hand trailed down her side, to her lower back, then to her bottom. He rubbed and gently squeezed her ass as he pressed his pelvis into hers. She lifted her leg, wrapped it around his waist, and writhed against him. Any more of that and Cam knew he'd lose what little self-control he had. He pushed her leg down, then, with one hand, gripped her hands together and raised them over her head. Dipping his head to kiss her neck again, he eyed her breasts and saw her nipples straining against her shirt. That was his next destination. He moved his lips down to her breasts and, through the fabric, took one nipple between his teeth and tugged.

"Oh, my God," she groaned. Jill yanked her hands from his grip and started to take off her shirt. Cam stopped her.

"No, ma'am. Not yet."

Her face was flushed, breaths deep. "You are quite the tease," she growled.

Cam wiggled his eyebrows. "You'll be rewarded for your patience."

Still kissing her, he moved his hands to her breasts, kneading them and pinching her nipples. Then Cam reached a hand under her shirt and caressed her belly. He slid his fingers under the waistband of her jeans but stopped when he felt the top of her panties. Cam stroked the skin there, not going any further. Jill arched against him, trying to drive his fingers in deeper. He pulled his hand out and began playing with the hemline of her shirt. Finally, Cam raised her T-shirt over her chest and pulled aside the black, lacy cups of her bra. Groaning at the sight of them, he licked the tip of one nipple, just enough for her to feel it then moved on to the other one. Jill took his head in her hands and pressed his face against her breast. He took the whole nipple in his mouth and sucked on it hard. She cried out, gripping his hair in her hands. Cam took her other nipple in his mouth, but this time, he began stroking her inner thigh and pussy over her jeans.

"Jesus Christ, Cam!" she breathed and unbuttoned her jeans. Kissing her, he pulled them down, taking her panties with them. He cupped her between the legs, feeling how hot and wet she was for him. She rubbed her clit against his palm in a desperate attempt for release. He removed his hand.

"No," Cam growled. "Not yet." Her shirt was still pulled over her exposed breasts. Cam unhooked her bra, tore her shirt off all the way, and flung both across the room. He stroked her naked body from neck to thighs. "God, you're beautiful," he murmured against her lips.

Not any wasting time, Jill reached up, unbuttoned his shirt, and pulled it from his body. She undid his belt and the button on his jeans and slipped her hand inside his underwear. Jill groaned at what she found there; it was long and thick. She fondled his cock with gentle strokes and gave the head a gentle squeeze. It was Cam's turn to nearly lose control as he thrust his hips under her touch.

Jill smiled. "No, not yet." She slid her hands around to his ass and slid his pants down. They crumpled into a heap around his feet, and he kicked them off so hard they slammed against the baseboards of a far wall.

Their kisses became frenzied, and unexpected wildness came over Cam. He wrapped his fingers in her hair and pulled, forcing her head backward, where he nibbled and growled against her neck. His passion for her was eating him alive; he had never wanted a woman this much. He lifted Jill, and she wrapped her legs around his hips. Cam walked to the bed and fell on top of her, resisting the urge to plunge himself into her wet center. Instead, he moved down her body and spread her legs apart. Jill moaned at what she knew was happening next.

Cam saw the wetness between her thighs and went about licking them clean of her juices. With his thumb and forefinger, he spread her lips open and licked all around the clit, then barely tonguing it, resisting the urge to apply pressure. Jill could take no more.

"Cam! Please! I need to cum!" she wailed and started moving her hand toward her pussy.

Cam grabbed her hand before she could get there. He looked up into her desperate, flushed face, enjoying the sight of her writhing in carnal agony.

"Please?" he grinned. "That's the magic word."

Then he pressed his tongue against her clit and flicked it up and down. Jill clutched the bedspread. "Faster. Go faster."

He obeyed. With a moan verging on a scream, Jill came hard. The intensity of the orgasm left her weak and shaking.

Cam moved up her body, sucking each nipple as he went. He cupped Jill's face in his hands. "I want to hear you do that again. Look into my eyes when you cum."

He slid the tip of his dick just inside of her, rooting around for that elusive spot. "Tell me when I hit it," he ordered.

It didn't take long for Cam to find it. "There! There!" she breathed. "Don't stop!"

He pressed himself in place and massaged it with the tip of his cock. His self-control was eroding; his dick throbbed, and balls ached, but he was determined to make her orgasm again.

Jill raised her hips and thrust herself against the tip. Cam saw the orgasm building in the anguish of her face. "Look at me. Look at me," he whispered. Her eyes flew open as came, the climax uncoiling from her belly and shooting down through her cunt to her inner thighs. Her legs quivered around him.

He gave her a deep kiss. "Dear God, that was worth the wait. So beautiful."

Jill grabbed his ass and pulled him into her. Cam cried out in agonized relief. She groaned at the feel of him inside her, her pussy still throbbing from the last orgasm.

"Fuck me. Hard," Jill demanded.

He was happy to give in. He pounded into Jill's pussy, racking her whole body with his thrusts. She wrapped her legs around his waist. Cam slid one hand under her ass and one hand under her neck, gripping her into place. She felt his nails dig into her flesh, but the pain was delectable. His desire for her was bestial and wanton; she thought she might pass out from lack of breath.

Cam winced. He was coming. His face was red and wet, and the cords of his neck stood out. He pressed his forehead against hers, staring into her eyes. As the orgasm overtook him, he threw his head back and cried out hoarsely, digging his fingers more into her skin.

Sated, he collapsed on top of her, trying to catch his breath. Then, Cam raised his head and looked at Jill.

"Jesus Christ," he whispered. "What have you done to me?"

Nora & Sam

- for my Sam.

Nora pulled on a lacy pair of dark blue panties, then stuffed her ample chest into the matching bra's molded cups. She shifted until she was satisfied and comfortable. Nora looked at her watch. An hour until she had to leave. Nora smiled. Plenty of time. She pulled out a top, pulled it on, then wiggled into a pair of jeans. She looked at her reflection in the mirror, smoothed her top, and wiped sweaty hands on her jeans. She was beyond nervous. She had contemplated canceling, but it had been a long time since she had been this excited. Or this nervous. Not even last weekend for her no-show. But this guy… she answered the question in his profile, "Anybody have the answer to adult dating?" She felt a connection already because she searched for the answer herself, and she said as much. They were at least the same generation, a refreshing change from the usual Millennials and older Gen Z that hit her up.

She checked her hair in the mirror for the hundredth time. She put on her lip gloss topping off her makeup, checked her outfit, and smoothed her top, again. Nora grabbed her bag. She bounced down the stairs, skidded to a stop as her mother stood in the living room, hands on her hips.

"What's in the bag?" she inquired.

"My laptop, just in case he doesn't show. You know, like the last guy," Nora replied. Not telling her there was a change of clothes and a few surprises… just in case he's into that.

"I see."

Nora smiled. She pulled out her phone and checked the time. She saw a text message and decided she'd check it in the car.

"I gotta go," Nora responded.

"Be careful."

Nora nodded, scratched her husky behind the ears as he investigated her bag. She bent down and kissed him. He sniffed her face. She smiled, touching her forehead to his.

"You're my good boy. I'll see you later. Take care of Grandma for me," Nora whispered. She bounded out the door.

Her phone chirped. She checked the texts and her date was on the way. She took a moment to send his name, picture, and phone number to her daughter with a short note that said she'd do a check-in tomorrow morning to let her know she was okay. It was the first time she had done that, but it was also the first time she knew she was staying the night for an "adult" date. The term was rather charming, and it made her smile.

Nora popped open the door to the hotel room. It was rather elegant, a couch under the window, a king-size bed, a desk with a lamp, plenty of outlets, and an armoire. It was much better than the hole where she stayed in Chelsea for a significantly larger price tag. Lower price tags were a big perk to living in the south.

"Thank you, late child support," she whispered.

She closed the door and set her bag in the nearest chair. She picked up the remote, contemplated the T.V. but put it back down. She sat on the bed, staring at nothing until her phone chirped. She pulled her cell out of her back pocket, check the text, and smiled. Setting the phone on the desk, she unloaded her laptop. Nora could get some work done while she waited since traffic from his direction was a nightmare, and he was running late. The fact that he was communicating with her added points in his favor.

Nora was knee-deep in editing when her phone chirped. She read the text and sent her reply, hoping he was stuck at a stoplight or traffic while texting. After trading a few messages, Nora got back to editing. Her phone chirped again, and she picked it up. She grinned as she replied. He was almost there. She grabbed the ice bucket, the key and set off in search of ice.

After discovering that the ice machine on their floor was broken, she asked at the front desk and was directed to the one on the first floor. When Nora returned to the room, he was at the door looking down at his phone, a messenger bag slung over his shoulder, a faded black flat cap on, a t-shirt with a design she couldn't see clearly without her glasses from this distance, and a shirt over that. It's as if he heard her soft footsteps on the carpet because he looked up when she was a few yards from him. He smiled, and she grinned like an idiot.

"Nora?" he asked.

"Sam?" she answered. "The ice machine up here is broken, so I had to go hunt one down."

She opened the door and let him in.

"Are you disappointed?" Sam inquired.

Nora set the ice down; Sam set his bag down on one end of the couch. She turned and looked at him.

"Not at all," she responded. She surveyed the salt and pepper scruff on Sam's face, his light green eyes slanted down at the corners, and the hat perched on his head. She was definitely not disappointed.

"I'm going to put this in the fridge," he held up a bag, "I like it better chilled."

"I'll take your word for it," Nora said.

Sam sat on the couch and fidgeted. She couldn't tell if he was nervous or if he just fidgeted out of habit. He must have felt the need to explain because he did. They shared the ice breaker kind of info. He said he was a Corpsman in the Navy and Nora's heart skipped a beat. She felt more comfortable with fellow veterans, and he was medical. They delved into current occupations. Sam revealed he went into nursing after his Navy gig and was now retired. Nora was impressed. Not because he didn't look like it, but she knew that being in the medical field was a true calling, and being a nurse... Nurses took a lot of shit. It was evident that he'd loved it. Nora had wanted to be a P.A., but she wasn't very... mathy. She told Sam that, and he kindly offered to help her if she decided to do that. If it meant more time with this gorgeous man, then she should probably do it.

Sam turned on some music. Another thing that made Nora glad that they were in the same generation, music selection. She didn't mind this music at all.

Sam poured her a glass of whiskey over ice. He handed it to her, and she took a sip. Then another. It was pretty good. She told him so. They talked some more, had another glass; when Sam noticed Nora's was empty, he sweetly asked her if she wanted another. Then, her stomach screamed in protest. It needed more than Crown Royal Apple Whiskey. They discussed food options and finally settled on Shotgun Dan's Pizza, which Nora ordered from their website.

Sam had to drive as Nora was in no condition. He took her hand, their fingers intertwined, and he kissed her. She felt like she was on fire, and it had nothing to do with the whiskey. Those simple, loving actions… she missed those. She hadn't realized how desperately she needed them. Nora was beginning to understand that her love language included touch as much as it did kind and thoughtful gestures. When Sam pulled back, he was just inches from her face.

"Sometimes women just need to be ravaged," he remarked.

"Yes, we do," Nora responded.

Sam let go and led the way to the elevator. Once they arrived in the lobby, he took her hand again. He pulled her through the lobby, hand in hand. Nora felt like she was in high school again. When he looked back at her, he smiled, and she felt like they'd been doing this forever. She'd never felt like that, not even with her ex, and they'd been married ten years.

Once back in the hotel and food in their bellies, they were on their third glass of whiskey, and Sam's For Folk's Sake playlist on Spotify provided the evening's soundtrack in the background… Nora bounced and swayed to the music until Sam took matters into his own hands. He grabbed her face and kissed her. Nora responded by wrapping her arms around him. She returned the kiss with equal passion. Clothes came off one item at a time until they collapsed on the bed. Sam sighed when Nora's breasts were finally exposed. He put each one in his mouth and suckled them in turn. Nora sighed under his touch, hoping that he didn't notice the goosebumps where his fingers had been. She ran her hands through his baby fine hair and, for a brief moment, was a wee bit jealous at the softness but wondered how she was lucky enough to have this smart, beautiful, sexy man in her company tonight.

Nora had missed the touch of a real man. That Marine prick was just a child compared to Sam. He slid her back on the bed and slid effortlessly into her. Nora gasped. The feel of his cock inside her dripping pussy, he fit perfectly as he thrust in and out between her thighs. He kissed her as he moved slowly inside. She moaned and tilted her hips; his cock pushed against the top of her cervix. He was so close to her g-spot, if she just tilted a little more… oh God. There it was. He thrust harder as she tightened her muscles.

"May I cum inside you?" he whispered in her ear.

"Yes, always," Nora gasped as she felt herself ejaculate. She felt his last few hard thrusts with a light throbbing in her pussy. She knew then that he'd finished. It was amazingly seamless for their first time being together.

He pulled out and laid beside Nora. She curled up next to Sam. She felt comfortable pressed against his body, his arm around her pulling her closer. That feeling of having done this forever crept back in. This time Nora let it linger before pushing it away. That feeling could get her into trouble.

Nora was almost asleep, but Sam twitched. She kissed his neck. He twitched again.

"Sorry," Sam whispered. "I don't usually sleep like this." He sat up and stretched forward. "My neck and back hurt all the time, and this is how I usually sleep. It's less painful."

Nora put her hand on his back and slid behind him. She gently pressed on either side of his spine, massaging up to his neck.

"Tell me if this hurts too much or if it starts to feel a little better," Nora said. She hadn't done this for anyone other than her daughter in a very long time. It didn't feel awkward. Again that feeling of having been with him forever… but how did he do that? As she massaged, she gently kissed his spine and his neck. The feel of his muscles under her fingertips, his flesh against her inner thighs. She could feel the moisture dripping from her pussy. She didn't remember this reaction from her body to any other man she'd been with. Sam leaned back into her. It was strange to her, but she was ready to go again.

"Are you ready for round two?" Nora queried softly as her lips brushed his ear.

"I don't know," Sam murmured.

Nora slipped her hand down to his cock. It was somewhere between hard and soft. She caressed it, admiring the effort Sam had put in to ensure he was cleanly shaven. She felt his manhood grow harder. Nora was curious about what he would taste like and how he would feel. She wanted to see if she could fit all of him in her mouth. She moved from behind Sam; he leaned back onto the pillows.

She kissed his chest, slowly working her way down to his beautiful cock. She ran her tongue over the tip, then gently took it into her warm mouth; one hand circled the base, squeezing following her mouth up and down, the other hand cupped his balls. She carefully kneaded them. Sam placed one hand in her hair, pushing her head down, and his cock fit nicely to the back of her throat. His other hand found her ass before a finger slipped inside her pussy. He worked the digit in and out, causing Nora to lose her focus for a moment. She stopped. Sam stopped.

He was hard, and it was time to ride his cock. Nora slipped a leg over his torso as he withdrew his finger. She took his hand. She cleaned his finger of her body's lubrication as she looked into his beautiful eyes. Nora bent down and kissed him deeply. She sighed, reached back, found his cock, and scooted back, sinking on to it. Nora rocked back and forth, rotating her hips in a figure eight. She leaned forward. Sam grabbed her breasts and rolled her nipples between his fingers. Nora gasped. She worked faster.

"Rollover on to your stomach," Sam breathed.

She did as requested. Sam came up from behind and entered her. Nora dropped from her hands to her chest, allowing Sam to enter deeper inside her. He thrust gently.

"Faster," Nora gasped. Sam obliged his hands on her hips, burying his perfect hardened sailor into her pussy. Nora gasped as she came. She didn't feel the throbbing from Sam that she had before. He kept thrusting; Nora tightened up her muscles again but felt herself cumming again.

"Oh, God," she moaned.

Sam's thrusts slowed, and he smacked Nora's ass. It wasn't what she was expecting, but it was lovely. He thrust in and out a few more times before Nora could feel his cock pulsing inside her. He pulled out and collapsed beside her. She kissed him.

"Congratulations," she announced, "you are on a shortlist of men," Nora curled up next to him again, hand on his chest, "that have been able to get me off and cum. For me, those are not mutually exclusive events."

Sam kissed her forehead. "I'm glad." He paused. "Do you mind if I smoke?"

"Nope, do what you have to do," Nora remarked as Sam slipped out of bed and retrieved a locked black case from his bag. "And I'm sorry, I probably should have told you, I have a ridiculously high sex drive." Nora watched Sam.

"It's okay."

She had trouble keeping her eyes off him. She didn't care that he's explained the muscle loss. His arms were working just fine. She enjoyed how they felt around her. She trembled under the caress of his hands. That was how a woman should feel with her partner.

Sam checked the pizza box. Pulled a piece out, took a bite, held it up, offering Nora a bite. She took it and chewed thoughtfully. He repeated the process until they had finished off the last two pieces.

"I hope you don't mind the M.J. I use it to help manage the pain. I do have my medical marijuana card, and it's a concentrate." He climbed back into bed. "I'll show you." He unlocked his case, pulled out a little torch, a pipe, and a small clear disk that reminded her of a petri dish. He unscrewed the top of the disk. "So, I heat the end of this," he proceeded to heat the pipe's narrow end, "then put it to this." He placed the warm end to the solid in the disk for a couple of seconds, then smoked it. He repeated this a few more times before he put it away.

Sam snuggled up to Nora. He kissed her forehead. They talked more, and Nora caressed his chest as she listened. He was smart. Sam spoke of ideas and issues rather than it being all about him. He let her respond with her view and opinions. She sighed. She could lay with him forever, and it wouldn't get old. She stretched out and slipped her leg over his; he moved his, and they were intertwined. She kissed his neck, collar bone, chest, and then worked her way back up to his ear, which she gently nibbled. His hand caressed her backside; the other hand found a breast and stroked it. She pressed her hot pussy into his thigh. Her hand found its way to his cock again.

"Round three?" she implored.

"Uh-huh," Sam groaned.

Nora slipped down and kissed his cock before she slipped him inside. She reveled in the moment and looked in his eyes as she rotated her hips. Those soulful eyes had seen so much pain. She leaned down, he thrust his hips up, and Nora moved up and down.

Sam put his arms around her and rolled over, but he slipped out of her. Nora readjusted, and Sam slipped back in. She sighed. He pushed in, Nora wrapped her legs around his waist, he grabbed one and put it over his shoulder. She pushed her hips up and felt him deeper.

"Oh, God," she gasped. "Give me more, baby."

Sam thrust harder and slower.

"Sam," she moaned, "You're making me cum."

Sam smiled at her. Nora groaned, and he thrust faster.

"Cum inside me, mmm, oh," she whispered breathlessly.

After a few final thrusts, Nora slipped her leg off Sam's shoulder, and his arms buckled. She wrapped her arms around him, helping him back to the bed. They laid tangled in the sheets. Sam mumbled some more brilliant ideas before disengaging himself and lighting up again.

"I hope I haven't worn you out," Nora prodded.

"Nah," he responded.

"Are you sure?"

"Sure," he protested.

Nora waited until he was finished smoking before curling up against him again. Damn, he felt so good. They both finally dozed off. Even Sam's twitching didn't bother her.

Nora woke up to light pouring through the curtain's crack that didn't shut all the way. She checked the time.

"Shit!" she hissed.

She kissed Sam's neck.

"Babe, I gotta go. You have time for round four before I go?" she solicited.

"I don't think so," he mumbled into the pillow.

"It's okay, babe," she kissed him again, then slid off the bed. She pulled a change of clothes out of her bag, changed, and quickly packed up her laptop. Nora climbed on the bed again. She stroked Sam's hair, kissed his shoulder, then his cheek. "I'm so sorry. I don't want to go, but I have to. Do you want me to leave a wake-up call for you for ten?" Sam sleepily nodded. She kissed him again, "This was amazing; thank you."

Nora stopped by the front desk. She caught the attention of the associate.

"Would you give room 449 at ten o'clock wake-up call, please? And if he checks out and tries to pay, don't let him. Leave it on the card on file," she requested.

"Yes, ma'am. We'll take care of that for you," the young lady replied.

"Thank you so much," Nora emphasized.

"You're welcome."

Nora grinned as she bounced out of The Crowne Plaza. He was terrific—an intellectual equal, not a drunk anxiety stricken crayon eater. One part of her brain was calculating how she could cultivate this into a longer relationship, while the self-doubt unconsciously started working on ways to self-sabotage the burgeoning relationship.

Nora sat in her car before she pulled out of the parking lot and sent a text message to Sam, thanking him for the evening, reiterating how amazing he had been. She smiled; her insides were all warm and fuzzy.

Nora sent a message to Sam, inquiring if he was available to come up to her place. He replied with an affirmative. She sent him her address, and she jumped in the shower. She shaved her legs and gave her undercarriage an excellent scrub to prepare for Sam's arrival.

As she dressed, she played his For Folk's Sake playlist on her Google Home. She selected a red satin and lace bra with a matching thong. Nora hoped Sam would appreciate her efforts to be sexy for him. Thongs were damn uncomfortable for her with her extra fluff. She put on jeans and a button-up shirt. She made sure one of her robes was handy, just in case she needed it. She put makeup on and looked at her hair. She let it air dry; her curls were more pronounced when she did that. She changed the sheets on her bed, running the dirty ones down to the washer. She pulled off her teddy bears and placed them in a plastic container by her closet. Her phone chirped. She pulled it out of her pocket and read the text. She grinned. He was in the driveway. Nora bounded down two flights of stairs and yanked open the door.

Sam got out of the car when he saw her. Hat and shades on his head. She smiled so hard, her cheeks hurt. She was hot, just seeing him.

"You made it!" she exclaimed.

"I did." He grinned.

Nora allowed him entry. He kissed her as the door closed, and the lock clicked. This time it was her turn to lead the way, his hand in hers. She didn't have any misgivings about him being here with her. She wondered if he knew the amount of trust she had in him to be here, in her home. But it didn't matter because he was here right now, and butterflies were in her stomach. She led him to her bedroom.

"I know, I have a kid's bed, but it's all that fits right now," she said.

"It's fine," he responded.

She stopped next to the bed. Sam pressed into her back, and she leaned into him. She missed this and him. Even though they'd only had the one night, and it had been a month and a half ago… this still felt so effortless. His profile was right. Adult dating was easy, but he was easy to be with.

Nora turned and kissed him. She tugged at his shirt, slipped her hands under it, and dug her nails in, dragging them down, around his ribs to his back. He let go of her and pulled back. Sam took his hat off, pulled his shirt up and over his head, it hit the floor. Nora kissed his chest as Sam fumbled with her buttons, but he got her shirt undone. It hit the floor next to his shirt. He slipped her bra straps down, exposing the tops of her pale, full breasts.

Nora placed kisses everywhere she could reach. She slipped her hands into his waistband; he undid his pants and shoved them down. Nora dropped to her knees and took his manhood in her mouth. Her hand went around to his ass, and she squeezed as she sucked.

Sam placed a hand on her head, gripping her hair. He groaned under her ministrations.

"Baby, I think I thought about this too much on the way here," he guided her off him. She stood, her shirt hung open.

"It's okay," Nora responded. She took off her jeans and sat on the bed. Sam sat next to her. She put her hand on his neck and lightly stroked the nape, letting her hands run through his hair. Still so soft. How does he do it? She could play with his hair all day.

Sam slowly laid back onto the bed, gently tugging Nora down with him. She wrapped her legs up with his. He was between her and the door, conveniently blocking her access to her pistol, but he didn't know it was there. If he did, he didn't mention it. However, she didn't think she'd need to defend herself against him. The fact that he was the only man she'd ever been with that had taken up that protective posture. Now that Nora thought about it, he did that in the hotel room, too. She immediately felt a surge of affection for him.

"May I smoke?" Sam requested after a while.

" Uhm, yeah, on the back deck."

"I'll be right back," he kissed her and got dressed. Nora pulled on her black satin robe. She made her way down the stairs to wait.

Sam soon reappeared at the front door, his messenger bag over his shoulder. He shut and locked it behind him. He put the bag down in the nearest chair, fished out his case, and followed Nora downstairs.

He leaned on the railing, popped open his case, and started his ritual. Nora watched him fascinated. His habit didn't bother her at all. Typically, smokers and drug users weren't her types, but all this about Sam… it didn't matter to her. She wanted to ask him if he was disappointed in her. He must not have been, or he wouldn't have been here. They got on so well. The flow from conversation to making love was effortless and precisely what she was looking for. When Sam finished, they retired upstairs to Nora's room.

They resumed their positions, chilling on Nora's bed. Her head on his shoulder, caressing his chest. They were chatting when Sam caught Nora off-guard.

"I love your company," he asserted.

Nora took a few seconds longer to process the comment than she should have.

"I really enjoy your company, too." She wanted to smack herself. She knew what issue posed the most significant risk to his sanity and well-being, and she didn't care. She wanted to be with him for as long as she could have him.

Sam was quiet for a few moments as he stroked her hair. Nora propped herself up on an elbow and gazed at him. A smile crept in. He grinned back at her. She pushed up, found his lips, her tongue darted past his parted lips, and they kissed passionately, tongues dancing. Sam reached down and tugged at her panties. She pulled away, took them off, then tossed them next to the bra. Sam unfastened his pants. He shoved them down.

Nora gripped his cock, guiding his sailor into her bay. Her robe hung open. Sam grabbed her breasts and sucked, hard, on each one. She moaned. Nora moved up and down, once again amazed at how well this worked for them. He moved with her, thrusting his hips up at just the right time, causing Nora to gasp. She could feel herself cumming, but neither of them had orgasmed yet. Nora had to satisfy him because he'd been so wonderful to her. She pressed into him, rocked back and forth, swiveling her hips in an oval pattern.

"Oh, Sam…" she breathed, followed by a soft grunt. She was cumming again. She squeezed her muscles and lifted ever so slightly, then back down. She repeated until he was close to release, then she pushed into his pelvis, and maintaining the pressure on his cock, rocked back and forth until he came, and she orgasmed.

Nora looked down at him, her bottom lip between her teeth. She broke into a grin when she saw the contentment on Sam's face. Nora kissed him. That moment… she didn't know how to describe what she felt. Bliss? Fulfillment? Happiness? That was so unfamiliar to her these days. She had forgotten how they all felt. Nora was on feelings overload.

She got up and looked Sam up and down, naked on her bed. That's where he should be more often. But with their situations…

"Oops. You got some blood there. Let me take care of that," Nora confessed. She hurried to the bathroom, grabbed a damp washcloth and a towel. She returned, cleaned him up, but wasn't awkward at all, unlike the Marine. It was kind of comical.

"Sorry, it was me," she continued.

"Well, if it had been from me, it would have been a problem," he chuckled.

"Give me a minute; I've got to go," Nora stated.

She grabbed her clothes and went back to the bathroom, where she hastily dressed. She cleaned herself up, then returned to her room. Sam was dressed, sitting on the edge of the bed. Nora straddled his lap. She sat, wrapping her arms around him, holding him tight. He hugged her. God, why did this have to end? Could she keep him? He made her feel appreciated, safe, wanted… this was what partners should feel like together. She rose, looked at him, leaned down, and kissed him. She liked how his lips felt on hers; their mouths made for each other. Nora pulled back. She stood in front of him, holding his hand.

"Why do I get the feeling you're trying to get rid of me?" he prodded.

"Unless you want to meet my mom…"

"Yeah, sure, why not?"

"Really?" Nora responded skeptically.

"No," he laughed.

"I thought so," she smirked.

Sam got up, grabbed her, and started dancing a two-step to the song playing. Nora laughed.

"I didn't know you could dance! I love to dance," she proclaimed.

"Dated a girl who could dance her ass off."

"I took ballroom dancing lessons with my mom in high school."

When the song ended, Sam hugged Nora. She melted inside. There was another hook in her heart. He now had six, just a few more, and she would be his, but did he know what he was doing to her? Is that what he wanted?

"I wish you didn't have to go," Nora whispered. She led him back to the front door. He kissed her again, then smiled that sexy smile. Damn, that smile, those eyes, his brain… she needed that.

"Bye, be safe," Nora said.

"Bye," Sam replied.

Nora watched his car pull away, and her heart broke. She was addicted to Sam if you can be addicted to people.

Every time Nora closed her eyes after that, all she could feel was Sam's lips on hers. The sensation of his touch was seared onto her skin. She could feel his arms around her. He told her he was in so much pain, and it hurt her to know that she couldn't help him, but she still loved him. He said he felt useless with each passing day because his arms were getting weaker. No matter how many times she told him he was perfect for her, he still wouldn't let her see him.

Nora prays for Sam every night. She tells him good night and good morning, just so he knows that someone out there loves him and misses him, just the way he is.

(Want to listen to Nora & Sam's soundtrack? Find their playlist on Spotify by searching playlists for Nora & Sam.)